MAKING MARKS IN THE SAND

AN ANTHOLOGY OF CONTEMPORARY SHORT STORIES

MAKING MARKS IN THE SAND

AN ANTHOLOGY OF CONTEMPORARY SHORT STORIES

First published in by Coverstory books, 2022

Paperback ISBN 978-1-8382321-7-7
ebook 978-1-8382321-8-4

www.coverstorybooks.com

Contents

Uncle Vee - Nigel Ferrier Collins 7

Devotion - Linda Davis..25

Christian's Dab Bay - Linda Davis...43

Saving Gracie - Polly East 63

After All This Time - Ian Gouge 73

The House We Lived In - Denise McSheehy 91

Grad Student Wife - Carol Park..101

The Vines - Yvonne Sampson 121

Dave's Vigil - Barbara Sapienza 141

✿

About the Authors 171

Recent publications from Coverstory books 177

Uncle Vee

Giles Writes

Cousin Michaela brought Vee into my life. She came to live with us in 1962 when my Aunt ran off to New Zealand with her fourth husband. Michaela was a highly strung and athletic fifteen-year-old. She ran Mum ragged. I was three years younger and regarded her as an exotic species. She shared a room with my sister Elena, which must have been quite an education for an eight year old.

Michaela started dating as soon as she legally could. She ignored her peers and went straight for men in their thirties, most of whom were probably married. She even brought some home, where they found themselves under polite but shrewd scrutiny from Mum. I remember an RAF officer who was loud and full of himself. There was a scruffy mountaineer who smelt bad. I also remember a TV presenter, whom Mum recognised. He was the oldest I saw; possibly early forties. Mum sized him up and sent him packing.

Late one Spring night Mum and I were trying to solve a thriller on the telly. We heard a throaty roar in the drive. Mum always sat near the front window so all she had to do was lift a corner of the curtain to see who was coming up the drive. I leaned over to look with her. We saw a long old fashioned sports car which discharged the sort of man whose shoulders have to go through doors sideways. He went round to the passenger side, but before he could open the door a bedraggled Michaela scrambled out and rushed into the house without saying a word. Mum was in the front garden in an instant demanding to know what was going on. She actually had her hands on her hips. When the man spoke he was calm and polite. I heard him ask if he could come in and explain. Mum pointed to the porch and in they came.

I thought I had better keep out of it and went to my room. It was only later that I was able to catch up. Michaela had been on a date at a country club in rural Kent. She was dancing with her current bloke when another woman came in and punched him in the face. The woman was screaming about two-timing etc. Michaela did a rapid fade. There was a fracas in the club and Michaela decided to leave the show altogether. She started off down a lane in the drizzle. Flashing blue lights across the fields sent Club patrons rushing for their own cars. She crawled through a gap in the hedge, tearing her little pink number in the process. The police and the exiting clients got into a stand-off in the lane and Michaela kept trudging away from the action with no real plan. She got to a slightly wider road with sporadic traffic. An open-top sports car stopped and a scary looking giant in a flying jacket asked her if she was OK. She fled and hid. He got out of the car and flagged down the next vehicle. It was a small saloon containing an equally terrified middle aged couple. He explained that he thought there was a girl in trouble nearby, but he had scared her off by mistake. Would they try and persuade her to get a lift? They wouldn't, and went on their way. Fortunately Michaela had been near enough to hear what was said and came out of hiding. She ended up accepting a lift in the sports car and was brought all the way home.

Mum was profuse with thanks, especially when she got him to admit how far off his route he had driven to deliver Michaela to our door. She also apologised for Michaela, who had gone to ground in her room. They had a brief chat which actually ended with Mum laughing and the man went on his way. He had said everybody called him "Vee".

About two weeks later I was daydreaming at the top of the giant willow in the garden when I realised that Mum was settling this man Vee into a deckchair on the lawn below. I swung down, via a show-boating route, to say hello. He engulfed my hand with his own. He had come back to see if Michaela was OK. She wasn't around as it happened, but we all thought on balance the answer was "yes". We drank ginger beer and chatted about this and that. Elena was very taken with "Vee" and persuaded him to paddle in her plastic pool. I noticed how delicately he did this, carrying his bulk nimbly like a dancer. Mum asked him where he worked. Mainly in London, he said, for the Government. He was a translator. What about sport, Mum asked, eyeing his physique.

"I wrestle" he said. "In the ring I'm Sir Martin Aston, an upper-crust villain".

He laughed, and so did Mum, who often watched the wrestling on TV with me. Vee had not yet been on TV but was due to fight Mike Marino in three weeks time in a televised bout from Croydon. Mum and I were impressed. We liked Marino.

"Who is going to win?" asked Mum.

"Good heavens!" replied Vee in mock horror "How could I possibly know?" and then he added "Actually I usually get disqualified" and grinned mischievously.

Vee asked if he could have a closer look at the willow tree. He did it to please me, no doubt, and it worked. He looked at the tattered rope that was my way up to the first bough. He clearly had his doubts. He took a few steps back and ran eight feet up the nearly vertical trunk and caught the lowest branch. I was not sure that I had really seen this, but that's what he did. We sat at the top of the tree and chatted. After a while he climbed down in a civilised manner, sprayed Elena with the hose, said something that made Mum threaten him with a flyswat, and left in his noisy sports car. It was as if he had been a lifelong friend of the family, and I was certain he would show up again.

Vee did show up again while Michaela was still with us. She flirted with him outrageously but he turned it into a burlesque. There was a moment when they danced on the lawn without Michaela's feet touching the ground. Then Vee turned his attention to Elena. Michaela got the message, eventually.

Vee continued to visit after Michaela left us. During my holidays a pattern emerged. He would arrive unexpected with a plan but wouldn't say what it was. It would simply transpire as we set off in his Allard open-top sports car. For example, it was high summer. I was fourteen and daydreaming around the orchard. Vee appeared dressed in a white blazer. When we got in the car I noticed my swimmers and a towel. I knew from experience that it was hopeless asking questions. I think he taught me a Finnish song which was about an old drunk fisherman who couldn't find the way home. The only swimming pool I knew about was in Lamerock Park, but we drove right past it. Vee pointed out a house by the park. It was an unusual, large, deco house with curved balconies. "Great place" he said.

Half an hour later Vee swung the car through a huge red brick gateway. A prominent notice told us we were entering a mental hospital. I knew I had been moody and awkward lately, but I thought this was a bit drastic. We stopped in a small car park reserved for staff. Vee put a sticker on the windscreen and led the way through what had once been a walled garden, under a yew arch, to a secluded swimming pool with stone seats all round. Actually the seats weren't what I noticed first; it was the nurses. And they noticed us, or rather Vee. There was immediate ribaldry. They all knew who Vee was, and were obviously pleased to see him. Someone showed me where to change behind a brushwood screen and by the time I emerged Vee was already poised on the edge of the pool. He entered the water with barely a splash. There was instant mockery and howls of derision. The nurses wanted to know what had happened to the "depth charge". Vee asked them if they wanted any water left and then obliged by re-entering, knees tucked, with the most enormous splash. He went under, but he didn't come up. As he had hoped all the women tried to rescue him.

Vee was good at inventing swimming strokes. My favourite was the not-waving-but-drowning stroke which involved swimming just under the surface with one hand waving limply above the water. We were making a lot of noise and I remember thinking we were behaving like lunatics. The whole pool was a froth. Somehow, in the midst of this frenzy, I spotted a young woman sitting beside the pool with her head in her hands. Vee must have seen her at more or less the same moment because he extricated himself from the wildness and went to sit down next to her.

The sun was quite fierce and Vee was dry in minutes. I found an oasis of calm in the pool and watched the infinite tenderness of his attention to this unhappy person. Neither spoke often, and he spoke less. He took her hand very gently and they just sat there for what seemed like a long while. Eventually she smiled wanly and came with him to the pool, which was now quietening.

I clambered out to sun myself and watch things from outside the pool. A nurse called Aileen came to sit next to me, which seemed quite thrilling at the time. I wasn't quite sure what to say so I asked her clumsily about Vee's connection with the hospital.

"I think he gives all his ring earnings to this place," she told me.

I sat and watched the restless aerobatics of red dragonflies and the shifting of cloud shadows on the pool. I stole the odd glance at Aileen. She looked to me like a goddess. The sad woman was trying to join in but you could see that she was distracted.

"She's homesick," said Aileen.

"Where is home?"

"Good question. She's Russian. Vee speaks good Russian. She likes that."

When we left Vee said goodbye individually to every single person.

"The nurses were nice," I said, in the car.

"So were the doctors," said Vee, with a smile. I had a lot to learn.

✲

I was sixteen. It was the Spring term at school. Vee had offered to take me out one weekend. I was glad of this because my parents almost never came. The mistake I made was to tell my friends about the outing and to describe Vee's car. They wanted to see this wonderful Allard. I found myself sitting on the stone wall outside the gothic library with four of the most cynical people I have ever known, waiting for Vee's grand entrance. There was the sound of a motorbike and we all looked up. It wasn't a bike, it was a three-wheeler like a large bubble car. "Here he comes" they joked, and I laughed too. But as the vehicle drew near I realised to my horror that it was indeed Vee.

I think I gaped. Vee waved. The laughter became mockingly raucous. I began to die inside. He pulled up by us and unwound himself from inside this absurd vehicle. My so-called friends cheered. Vee came over and shook everybody's hand.

"I thought you were bringing the Allard," I said, hoping at least that he would confirm that he had one.

"This *is* an Allard," he grinned. "It's an Allard Clipper".

I looked the front. It was an Allard.

Vee brought out some bottles of coke, opened them with his teeth and handed them round.

"Anybody want to take it round the block?"

Predictably Terry was up for it, and after a very brief tutorial (vehicles hold no great mystique for a farmer's son) he set off. Being Terry he wanted to see how well it cornered and nearly tipped it. Vee didn't bat an eyelid. He was looking at the great grey stone school buildings.

"Prison," said Alisdaire

"You think so?" said Vee

After what seemed like an age Vee extricated me from my compatriots and we chugged off up the drive. I was a bit sulky, thinking I had lost face. Actually I later discovered that Vee had made a very favourable impression on all and sundry. We went about a mile and Vee turned off the main road. There, with a small trailer, was the big Allard.

"Did you bring this three-wheeler all this way just for a joke?"

"We're going to deliver it to somebody who needs it, and then we are going to visit a hermit."

I had looked forward to Vee's visit so much and I was becoming quite despondent. I think Vee pretended not to notice. We got the Clipper onto the trailer and set off in the big red monster. Despite myself I began to enjoy it. In those days it was still a pleasure driving round minor roads in an open-top car, especially in the West Country. I was almost disappointed when we pulled up outside a Police house and a little girl came rushing out to say hello, closely followed by a rather haunted looking mother.

Vee unhitched the trailer and offloaded the Clipper. The mother, Jennifer, made us very welcome but the house had an air of neglect. From the way Vee asked her how she was, it was clear that some tragedy had recently occurred. The little girl looked at Vee in a longing sort of way. It was quite a difficult visit.

"Her husband was killed in a car chase" said Vee when we were on the road again. "There is an enquiry. The three-wheeler is cheap to tax and run. It'll tide her over."

We sped off in silence until we were well up into the Quantocks. Vee turned off along an unmade road, driving very slowly because the car was low sprung and the trailer tended to bounce. Eventually we came to a somewhat dilapidated cottage. It was literally in the middle of nowhere. It was even hard to see why it had ever been built there. The top of a stable type door opened and there was the image of an archetypal hermit. He had long black hair, a beard, burning dark eyes.

"Go away!" he shouted, but there was a smile on his face.

"Nipun this is Giles, he's on parole from boarding school."

"No good will come of it" said Nipun. "Come in if you must."

I expected to see a room cluttered with inexplicable objects (even fetishes). Instead all was orderly and clean. Bare wood table, rafia mats, empty sink, neatly stacked plates. We went through into the day room and it was the same story. Sofa with clean drape, cane chair with decent cushion, desk with piles of papers squared off and held in place with clear glass paperweights. Vee couldn't stand up straight under the beams.

"I have beer," said Nipun "Do you drink Indian beer Giles?"

I looked at Vee for a cue, but he was watching a bird which had settled on the window-sill.

"Yes please," I said.

While we were sipping our drinks Nipun got up and seized a folder from his desk.

"This might interest you," he gave it to Vee.

Vee opened the folder and instantly nothing else seemed to have his attention.

"Come and see my croquet lawn," said Nipun and led the way through an unpainted door into a very overgrown garden. At first it was impossible to see how croquet could be played in such an environment, but then I realised that it was criss-crossed with mowed tracks. At the junction of each track was a hoop. Nipun handed me a worm-eaten mallet and ball and battle commenced. My first few hits went straight into the jungle.

"Try this," suggested Nipun. He stood to attention mallet raised. "Rule Britannia!" he roared and belted the ball straight down the middle of a track. I tried it, and my next shot was going straight for the hoop until it hit a mole hill a yard from it.

"That mole hill wasn't there when Nipun took his shot."

I looked round. Vee was standing there with a mallet in one hand and the folder in the other.

"He trains the moles you know." As he said this he belted his ball down the track with one hand. It hit the hoop and knocked it out of the ground.

"Treasonous shot!" announced Nipun "Ten points against."

"Have you shown this to anyone?" asked Vee waving the folder.

"Not yet."

"I am sure the Department will buy it," said Vee and strolled down the track to take a shot which sent my ball on a journey into the briars. "Sorry," he said, unconvincingly.

"Machete time-out," announced Nipun, and produced said implement.

In the process of finding my ball we discovered a statuette of a nymph, a rusty old trap, and the sloughed skin of a grass snake. Later ball retrieval yielded a rotten sandal, an enamel door number, a brass poker, a stone bird-bath, and a doll's eye. We placed these on a stone wall near the cottage and Nipun awarded points for each item. He declared the whole contest a draw.

"Only a mathematical genius could create a draw out of eight divided by three," said Vee.

"Tea-time," replied Nipun.

I don't remember much about the meal but at one stage Nipun asked me if I enjoyed Maths. I told him that to me it was a complete mystery. He said something like:

"Mathematics is the only universal language. Those who try to stifle or discredit it are the true enemies. Even if you are not a mathematician you must fight those enemies."

Apart from that I do remember laughing and hoping a day like this might happen again. Later, when Vee dropped me back at school, I didn't even care that nobody saw the red monster.

✿

The number and duration of events escapes me now but key moments spent with Vee are etched. A half-hearted police raid on an unlicensed Limehouse blues cellar in the middle of a wonderful set by Roosevelt Sykes; exploring a disused railway tunnel with a very intense photographer called Alfonso; a raucous birthday party on board a docked Norwegian freighter...some of the best moments of my life before I met Claire. I will get round to setting some of them out one day. Vee only belongs to my youth, but his influence has been with me ever since. He said to me once:

"If you want to get close to people focus on their uniqueness. If you want to help society, focus on what people have in common." That has been the basis of my career.

Claire Writes

You would think from my husband's writing that he came from a one parent family. There is no mention of his father, who must surely have been around on some occasions. He was not one to remain quiet in a corner, so what did he make of Vee, and vice versa? Giles doesn't say in his piece and he didn't connect Vee and his father in conversations with me over the years.

You will notice that the Vee episodes appear to end when I come on the scene. This is more or less correct. I never met the man. Giles talked about him more than his family during the first years we were together and I was quite sceptical about some of the stories I heard. I have older brothers so I was used to young male hero-worship. I also realised early on that Giles has a preoccupation with size. Largeness and robustness get his attention every time. He had a picture of a dashing wrestler on his wall when we met, and for a long time I thought it was Vee. It turned out to be someone called Joe Cornelius. When I finally saw a picture of Vee, in his ring persona of Sir Martin Aston, the thing that struck me most was his intelligent eyes.

I say that it is more or less correct that the Vee episodes ended when I came on the scene. In actual fact there are two very important episodes missing from the account which post-date my arrival. Giles actually met Vee fifteen years after he and I were together. He never told me because he shouldn't have been where he was at the time. I found out because I suspected that Giles was having an affair. In 1981 all the signs were there. Odd patterns of work; signing up for a lot of residential training; too much detail about where he had been; moodiness; post picked up the minute it hit the doormat. I gradually realised that I knew who it was. It was the daughter of one of my mother's best friends. We'll call her Sofia.

Sofia was, and still is, a clever and likeable person. She was quite young when Giles took up with her. Because of her youth, and the impression that there was a strong bond between them, I saw a potential threat to my marriage. I decided to ask her what she was planning to do with my husband. She lived in London and I arranged to meet her. I suggested a public place and she chose a cafe near Covent Garden. We had met before, at her parents', but this time I saw her through my husband's eyes. I understood the attraction. Sofia had an aura of energy, and communicated with her whole body; but her dark eyes were steady and deep. She didn't apologise and she was tactful about details; but she did not deny that she and Giles had been more than just friends. She said she was very fond of him and thought she might have been in love. When they started seeing each other privately she had been at a low ebb. He had been helpful and she felt she had found herself during their relationship.

She told me that things had changed because of a chance encounter with an old friend of Giles'. Two months before my meeting with her, Sofia had arranged a fleeting liaison with Giles in that very cafe. He did not have much time and the idea was to have a quick meal together. About halfway through their meal this friend of Giles's came over to their table. Giles had greeted him warmly but very nervously. She found the friend respectful and attentive and she had invited him to sit with them. Within seconds they were all three talking jovially about nothing in particular. Then Giles had to leave. He said his farewells and left her with the friend. After a while the man had said: "Time to move on, perhaps." At first she had assumed it was his way of saying he had to go; but he let the words linger too long for that and she realised he was trying to tell her something. As they talked further she realised that when people from different generations fall in love, one is often looking for something they never had and the other is looking for something lost. At the point where one or both realise that the search is futile and unnecessary it is time to move on.

Vee told her he knew about her research translating the Imatra Codex and he left her a contact number for someone who might have some interesting work for her. By the time Sofia and I met she had followed this up and had a second interview pending. She told me that, in a few kind words, this stranger had brought her face to face with some uncomfortable truths. She planned to tell Giles that their relationship needed to change, or end. I believed her. She promised to let me know how she was getting on with her new life, and we parted on friendly terms. Her description left no doubt in my mind that the stranger had been Vee.

Sofia has been as good as her word. She contacts me from time to time and visits us. She cannot say exactly what she is doing but I gather she is some kind of cryptographer and that she enjoys it. Giles knows nothing of my first meeting with her. He was clearly cut up by the end of the affair but I could see that he genuinely wished Sofia well.

The other episode happened after Giles wrote his potted account of Vee. Our grand-daughter, Alicia, is on a gap year in Scandinavia. It is not clear to me what she is up to, but it seems to be interesting for her. About two weeks ago we tried to set up a Skype with her but the dog ruined the webcam her end, so she sent us a long Email.

Alicia's Email

Hello Grannie and Grandpa, sorry about the Skype fiasco. The dog is normally quite placid. Since I last wrote I decided to go to a place called Äteritsiputeritsipuolilautatsijänkä in Finland because of the cool name. Everybody said there's nothing there, but that's true of most places in Finland. Anyway, it's a boggy area with nowhere to stay so I took a bus to the nearest village with a hostel. After two days I had to admit it was boring even by back-packing standards; and then I met Ukki and Maalia in a sort of shop. Now I'm staying with them and it's like someone turned on the lights. They are lovely people, so full of energy but calm and reassuring. I think they're probably in their early thirties but they haven't given up on anything. Everyday I learn from them. I think you would like them.

This cabin of theirs is quite remote. It used to be Maalia's family's holiday home but U & M live in it all year now. They are translators and can work from anywhere. It's very beautiful here. I've put some photos on my site. The main reason I wanted to talk with you is that we had a visitor who will interest you I think. We were painting the outside of the cabin when a truck came and some really rough people got out. U & M didn't know them and I think they were a bit nervous, but then an old old man got out and Maalia went straight up and hugged him. I thought he must be family. The others went off in the truck and left the old man with us. I could see he was staring at me and I did think he should know better at his age but I shook his hand (which was twice the size of mine) and I stopped feeling annoyed with him straight off.

U went in to make coffee and this man picked up a paintbrush and started to paint the cabin. M tried to stop him but he was well into it, and doing it better than us, so we painted together while she asked him how he was.

"Good enough for what I have to do." That was when I realised he was English. And then he said "Those ne'er-do-wells are probably off to do some mischief so I thought I'd stay with you to get an alibi".

He was like that the whole time, you didn't know when he was kidding. He made us all laugh a lot but you couldn't take your eyes off him. He said his name was Vee and he lived about a hundred kilometres further North with some Reindeer herdsmen. He didn't call them that but Ukki explained the words he used that way. Every now and then I realised he had just said something like: "Language is growing faster than humans can grasp" or "Lives are not stories; they have an ending but not a plot" or "Never trust a god that hides" and "they say that it is more important to travel than to arrive, but if you are alert on a journey it is an infinite number of arrivals." I noted some more of these on my phone.

Anyway, on the last evening he told me he knew who I was (I was like get me out of here!) and he had a message for my grandfather and my great aunt. When I was feeling less paranoid I gave him Aunty Elena's address and I think he is going to send her something. This is the message for you, Grandpa:

Vee says he wishes he could have met Claire and the rest of the family, but it became best that people couldn't connect you all with him. He remembers lots of fun times with you Grandpa and he always knew you would know what you had to do with your life. He has followed your career from a distance. He was very sorry to hear about Great Granny dying. He knows this type of message after all these years is hopeless but he wants you to know that he is basically well and expects to die while herding reindeer. I think this was a joke, but I'm not quite sure. He wants you to go to The Beige House (he says Aunty Elena will know what he means) and talk to the owner. He has asked her to give you something ~ he wouldn't say what.

I've got to say this guy is not at all normal. For one thing I don't think he sees the world like other people. Maalia and Ukki say he is an amazing linguist and although they grew up in Finland Vee knows more about some aspects of Finnish culture and dialects than they do. They obviously adore him and were very sad when he had to go after three days. I suppose when people get to his age you are never sure if you will see them again. I won't, which is a bummer. Grandpa if you are as fit as Vee is when you are that age!!!

I must tell you about the people who came to pick him up. I said they looked rough when they dropped him off, and they still looked a bit wild when they came for him, but they had cleaned up and were wearing quite smart stuff. The thing was though, they treated him like a celeb. They actually lined up outside the cabin like an escort and when he climbed up into the truck they shook hands with all of us (it took ages) and roared off hooting the horn and waving out of the window. Ukki said:

"Did we just watch a rescue or a kidnap?"

Maalia said: "It was a reunion, but imagine what is going to happen when he gets back to the wives and daughters!"

I'm so glad I met this man and you were very lucky to go around with him Grandpa. Don't forget to go to The Beige House.

It will be hard to leave U&M but as soon as we have finished the painting I think I should move on. I'll keep you posted. By the way, just before he left I asked Vee for some advice for my travels. He said: "Be. Enjoy. Give." I asked if that was all, and he added "Avoid gurus and people with cold eyes."

Lots of love, A (XXX)

Elena writes

I like my brother Giles, but there is a distance between us. We didn't really grow up together because he was away at school for three quarters of the year. Because I was six years younger than him there was always a sense of tolerance or patronisation. You can see it in his account of the Vee episodes. Vee is there for him. I am an extra.

In actual fact, and I have never bothered to point this out to Giles, I saw more of Vee than he did. So did Mum. He used to come round when Giles was away. I called him "uncle" because that's what you did with adult friends of the family; but it was also how he behaved. He was good fun. He played games with me, helped with my homework, and even came to see my dancing displays. I taught him to do the splits (mind you Mum had to come and help him back out of one ~ much hilarity). He took an interest in Mum's costume making and brought her some photographs of traditional costumes in parts of the world he had visited. Dad liked him too, I think. But Dad always needed to be the centre of attraction, and that was difficult when Vee was around.

Giles has always had this great need to feel that his life was special so we let him believe what he liked about Vee. When you look at what Giles says about Vee, and I have noticed this in other aspects of Giles' life, you realise that he was hopeless at asking the pertinent question. For example, he says that Vee used to come round unexpected, with an undivulged plan, and off they would go for fun and frolics. It never occurred to him that Mum would never have allowed this. He never asked if she knew about it all, and approved the plan. During term time I occasionally heard them talking about what Vee might cook up for Giles in the holidays. There was no mystery, even to the visits to old blues singers in dingy clubs. Mum knew all about it and she knew she could trust Vee.

Giles writes as if we were all satisfied with the answer to the question of what Vee did for a living (apart from part-time wrestling). Well Giles may have been, but Mum and I are far too inquisitive. Vee worked for the Government and was fluent in Russian (and other languages) and wouldn't say more. Mum put it together intuitively and I got confirmation when I was head-hunted by the Home Office. Only Vee could have pointed them in my direction. The interview made clear that the work on offer was to do with national security. I was flattered but I turned it down.

When Giles is at the hospital swimming pool he asks why Vee acts like he belongs there. He seems quite satisfied with the answer about giving ring earnings to the hospital benevolent fund. But he doesn't ask why Vee chose that hospital. I'm much too nosey (Vee used to tease me about it). Eventually I found out that Vee's mother spent her last nine years in that mental hospital. Giles asks about a sad woman. It doesn't occur to him to ask why she doesn't go back to Russia if she is homesick. I discovered that Lubya's father was a political prisoner.

I particularly like the description of the visit to the "hermit". Nipun Gill was a theoretical linguist. It was a branch of logical philosophy he practically invented. Some of his work is still said to be classified because it has a bearing on "intentionality in deliberately obfuscated communication". In other words, secret messaging. At the time, hardly anybody knew Gill was in the country and Giles actually meets him. He gives us a description of a croquet game played while Vee is reading a piece of original and unpublished work by Gill. Classic!

I don't know what Claire makes of Vee. I think she finds Giles' stories about him a bit trying. It was she who showed me Giles' brief Vee memoirs. With his permission I hope! She says she has written something herself but now realises she can't show anyone. I have my own memories of Vee and I have often wondered why he bothered with us as a family. My conclusion is that his work did not allow room for an ordinary domestic life. So, when fate gave him a way through to ordinary folk he took it, and for a while it offered him the nearest thing to domesticity that he thought was safe. We were special to him because we were ordinary.

Claire has asked me if I will go with Giles this afternoon to The Beige House near Lamerock Park to collect something Vee wanted Giles to have. I've already had a farewell package from Vee; a beautiful traditional Sami costume. I might tell Giles this, but I won't tell him what I know about The Beige House. He will meet Claudine who is the daughter of Lara (actually Doris) the lady who ran this house as a sort of private club (called Strays) for nearly three decades. It attracted musicians, dancers, artists, rascals, and eccentrics with its offbeat atmosphere and legendary "special events". Politicians and priests were banned. Strays features in several biographies. For example, the saxophonist Stella Arthur is quoted as calling it her "dream sanctuary". The artist Rory Fynde is said to have referred to it as "joyous borderline bedlam". The sound poet Heinrich Offen described it as "a hideout for the outer fringes of the avant-garde". My friend Suzie, who used to work there, said she taught Vee to merengue (despite ludicrous differences in height), and in return he taught her how to blind-side a referee. A full length biography of Vee himself is surely impossible. His life was like his description of The Beige House as a place where "special moments were shared while secrets were kept".

Claudine will hint about such things and about Vee's long-standing friendship with her mother. Giles will accept superficial information. He won't hear the stories of Strays' exuberant heyday. Claudine will take us to the garage. Giles will get very excited because he will begin to guess that he might be about to own an Allard. I wish I could see that broad grin on Vee's face when Giles realises which one it is.

Devotion

3:29 a.m.

"Looks like I have ovarian cancer," Lauren's mother, Nancy, said to her in a peevish voice, the one she used when she'd chipped a nail or couldn't find an earring. Lauren had gotten the call five weeks before, but the words have woken her up several times a night ever since.

3:31 a.m.

Lauren wakes to see six-year old Christian standing beside her bed, naked, half-asleep and smelling of urine. She vaults up and sets him down in bed, next to his father. In a minute, she returns from her sons' room with a dry set of pajamas and pulls the clean shirt on him. She leaves the pants. Too much work. She does all of these things at the same time as if trying to trick herself that she's still asleep. If she were a radio, the dial would be in-between stations, maybe a point away, where she can faintly hear voices but mostly static.

She lies down in her other son Ethan's bed, in the next room. Ethan is also in bed with her husband, Mike, and now, of course, Christian. Every night, at some point, one or both of the twins come into their bed. "A phase," she and Mike have been calling it for six months. Her bed is like a game of musical chairs, where she is always the one left without a chair.

Ethan's bed is the "space" bed. The sheets, the comforter, a poster, and a mobile above her are all in galactic motif. Pluto, the non-planet, looms close to her nose as Lauren lies, propped on Mercury and Uranus pillows. She names the planets, one by one, to ease herself back into sleep. Christian's bed, across the room, has a sports theme — assorted balls: soccer, baseball, and football. From where she is lying, Lauren can make out a pee stain the size of a manhole cover on the blue/black sheets and Christian's pajamas rolled in a ball on the floor. Laundry again tomorrow. With that thought, she closes her eyes and soon is back asleep.

4:29 a.m.

"R-EOW, R-EOW!" the cat meows from somewhere far away, but not far enough. Lauren leaps out of bed, again. She hurries by her bed in the adjoining room, with her husband and six-year-old twin sons in it, through to the hall where she finds the cat. The elderly white cat follows her down the stairs meowing the whole way, in spite of Lauren's attempt to shush it with an outstretched foot. "Outside. That's where you're going. I am not feeding you," she whispers to the cat. "No way. I won't have you getting used to eating at this hour."

Lauren opens the back door, places the cat on the porch, then returns inside and lies down on the living room couch to fall back asleep a third time. But her mind feels as crowded as a sold-out sports arena. There are the usual details of the day, but all thoughts lead back to her mother: the softness and perfumed smell of her skin, her child-like love of holidays, how they've been best frien..STOP! A hexagon shaped stop sign butts up to the edges of Lauren's mind. Thinking of her mother this way (grieving?) feels like a luxury, one that Lauren cannot afford. She must think of logistics. Her mother's recovery from recent surgery, the chemo ahead, which, in practical terms means: who will take Christian to his sports practice while Lauren takes Ethan to piano? Who will babysit on Saturday nights? Whom will they take with them on vacation next month in place of her mother?

4:33 a.m.

Resigned to staying awake, Lauren turns off the heat. She and Mike forever argue about the temperature in the house, the car, hotels. When Lauren is hot, Mike is cold, and vice-versa. After she turns down the thermostat, Lauren washes her face, pours moisturizer into her palm, then smooths the aloe smell onto her skin. The two lines between her eyes that look like a quotation mark. Her mother has the same lines, only deeper. As Lauren has watched her mother's body age, she sees it as a blueprint for her future: the poor eyesight when she was a child, her first period at 15 — later than all of her friends — the aching, arthritic joints in her late twenties, and the premature gray hair in her thirties.. With the news of her mother's cancer, she immediately made an appointment with her gynaecologist. "A hysterectomy after menopause should be a priority," the doctor calmly said, as if he were prescribing aspirin.

The cat comes back into the house through the pet door. She looks at Lauren and meows. Every time Lauren walks near the kitchen, the cat follows her and meows louder. She made the mistake of giving the cat cheese nine months ago after she learned that the black and bloody edge of the cat's ear was not from a fight, as she had thought, but cancer. "White cats have no pigment and are usually drawn to the sun," said the vet, whose office stunk of sick animals and the cleansers that failed to mask them. Nancy, ironically named after her mother, had shaken with fear on the metal examination table. "Both my Nancys have cancer," Lauren jokes with friends, as if she actually finds it amusing.

The sun is just rising as Lauren walks to her mother's nearby apartment to water her plants and retrieve her mail. The apartment still smells like overripe fruit, though it's all been thrown out. She cannot look at her mother's belongings - the photographs of Nancy with the kids on trips, her clothes, and an entire bookshelf of suspense thrillers - without thinking the worst, as though her mother's ghost is already inhabiting her home.

6:35 a.m.

Lauren is back home eating breakfast when the cat throws up. She sits reading, trying to ignore what's lying on the floor less than ten feet from her.

The cat jumps up and plops herself down in the center of the paper Lauren's reading. Lauren stands and scoops up the cat's mess with a fistful of baby wipes, her half-eaten oatmeal left behind. Of course, the cat had to get sick on the carpet instead of the floor, she thinks. She imagines the cat conspiring to do whatever is the most work for her; in the mind of an eighteen-year-old, diseased cat, work equals love. She walks into the kitchen to throw the mess in the trash. The cat follows. "*What* do you want from me?!" Lauren asks the cat impatiently, hands on hips. The cat squeaks as if to say, *We're compatriots in this effort to get me fed every second of the day*, instead of mortal enemies, which is what Lauren is feeling. She puts away the pots from last night's dinner, pours herself a cup of tea, and leaves the cat with the malignant ears standing there, waiting.

7:19 a.m.

Lauren prepares the kids' breakfast and lunch. Mike walks into the room and over to her. Their glasses touch when they kiss. "Cheers," he says, and yawns. "I've been up since 6:30. You do know that pots and pans are used for percussion, right?" Lauren lifts and drops her shoulders in an at-least-I'm-still-functioning-shrug. Mike puts water in the coffee pot. He's wearing a v-neck t-shirt, boxers, and suede slippers. His straight, skinny legs look like sign posts upon which his broad torso rests. Lauren has to maneuver her way around him to lower the heat on the kids' pancakes and back again to turn off the toaster oven. He yawns. Mike always refers to his life as "hard," though as far as she can see it's anything but. His parents spoiled him. He was rebellious, did drugs, grew his hair long, and fronted a moderately successful band. When he turned thirty-two, he traded in the band for an A&R job at a record company where he's now an executive vice president. The "hard" part, as far as she can tell, was quitting the drugs.

Lauren regards him a moment then turns away. Since her mother's illness, she's been holding his overweight parents, who live in Boca Raton and have barely seen the twins since birth, against him. Why couldn't it have been *his* mother? She thinks.

"The best grandmother," and "I want one of her," is what she consistently hears about her mom.

Mike clicks the thermostat on to a low hum. "I'm going to turn the heat up a bit."

8:15 a.m.

"Hurry!" Lauren shouts again to Christian, whom she is taking to school. The kids go to different schools, mostly because, academically, Ethan is so far above Christian, and Lauren and Mike don't want Christian to feel inferior. Christian ignores her first five pleas to stop listening to his iPod and get out of the car. Like his dad, he is obsessed with music. "Puff the Magic Dragon" and "Bohemian Rhapsody" are on his current playlist.

"Christian, please!" Is there anything slower than a slow child? Lauren wonders. Finally, he moves out of the car, looks around at the other families in the parking lot, and glares at her. "Mom! You don't have to yell. My friends probably heard you."

Lauren thinks of her sick mother and wants to scream. Then she reminds herself that he's only six; that he has no sense of what's going on other than Nana has not been around and the one piece of information he has hung onto: she will be losing her hair.

"I'll race you to the door, slow poke." She jogs ahead. As slow as Christian is at coming when called, he can't resist a competition, anything where he has the potential to win.

8:49 a.m.

Lauren does several errands before an 8:30 fundraising meeting at Ethan's school. Ellen waves to her when she walks into the conference room and pats the empty seat beside her. She's the last one to arrive. Is she the only one in the world with a hectic schedule?

"You okay?" Ellen whispers. She's sitting cross-legged on the carpeted chair, wearing Birkenstocks with black socks. Her hair is so long it's grazing her ankles.

"I feel like I've lived a whole day, and it's not even nine o'clock yet."

"Christian wet again?"

Lauren nods.

"Since having kids, I wet my pants all the time, too."

Lauren laughs.

The meeting drags on, and Lauren has to go grocery shopping before visiting her mother. "Let me know if I miss anything," she tells Ellen as she slinks out of the room, trying to make herself invisible.

The school office is adjacent to the conference room and on the way out, Lauren picks up *Vanity Fair* and *Time* magazine when the receptionist isn't looking and stuffs them into her oversized handbag. Ever since her mother has been in the hospital, she's been stealing magazines from offices all over Los Angeles.

At the grocery store, the line to the parking lot is, well, a parking lot. Lauren flips through *Time* while she waits in her car for a spot.

Ellen calls.

"Did I miss anything?"

"If it went on a moment longer, I might have done something awful."

"How do less sane parents handle it?" Lauren asks.

"Prescription drugs? Hey, how's Nancy?"

"I told her I'd be there at 10:00, and I still have to drop the groceries off at home." It amazes Lauren how glib she can be on the outside when, on the inside, even the mention of her mother's name makes her feel like she has a bowling ball in her abdomen. Her mother's doctor had said the tumor had spread outside her ovaries and was butting up against the small and large intestines. Lauren imagines the tumor he removed, black and decaying like the edges of the cat's ears. She feels a pain in her pelvis — real or imagined? She can't tell.

"Is there anything I can do to help?" Ellen asks. "Reflexology? Reiki?"

Lauren suggests Ellen take over a job she signed up for the fundraiser.

"Sorry darling. I'd do anything for your mom, but I do more than enough for that damn school."

10:19 a.m.

The late-morning traffic is typically not bad, unless, like today, there is road work being done. Lauren weaves her way through side streets to get to the hospital. By the time she arrives at UCLA, she feels like she just stepped out of a pinball machine. She spends ten minutes looking for metered parking, since the cost of parking in the hospital is expensive day after day. There's the inevitable rummaging for quarters and then the long walk from where she parked to the hospital. As she walks, she looks up at the building, pictures approximately where her mother's room is and the distance between them. She tries to convince herself that regardless of what happens, her mother will live on inside her, but she knows otherwise. Like the building before her, if the foundation is removed, the building will crumble, and, though it might be rebuilt, it will never be the same again.

11:00 a.m.

Lauren smells the hospital before she's inside.

"Knock, knock." She stands at the door to her mother's shared room. Lauren is relieved that her mother's roommate Pat is not there. A single middle-aged woman with lymphoma who has a bed full of stuffed animals, Pat is obsessed with Hollywood stars, and, after her mother bragged about all the stars she'd met through Mike's work, sees Lauren as her personal Make-a-Wish Foundation. "If you could ever get Neil Diamond to visit, I'd do cartwheels across this room," Pat said. If her mother wasn't ill, Lauren would remind her not to talk about Mike's job. People often mistook that sort of conversation as a personal invitation.

Her mother is sitting up in a chair. Her post-surgery stomach resembles a six-month pregnancy. "From trauma and IV fluids," the doctor had said. The hospital lighting makes her look green. Her calves are the size of small tree trunks from edema, but her hair is neatly styled, nails freshly painted, and she is wearing triangular Aztec earrings that color-for-color match her hospital gown. Her mother has always been big on color coordination. The house Lauren grew up in Elkins Park, Pennsylvania, had a bright red matching roof and door. "I'm a big disappointment to my mother," Lauren sometimes jokes. "I haven't worn a primary color since I was twelve."

"Hi, honey. How're the kids?"

"Good. Missing you." Lauren bends down and kisses her mother and smells chemicals, scalp and urine.

"I miss them too."

"How are you?"

"Better now that I got cleaned up. This morning I wet myself because they took so gosh darn long to come when I called to go to the bathroom. I can't stand the smell." She indicates her bed and the floor below, where she had her "accident." The smell. A small woman wearing a surgical mask, gloves, and a pink hairnet comes in to clean.

"Maria, this is my daughter."

"She is talking all the time about you." They watch Maria clean. Soon, powerful cleanser smells pervade the air. "I take good care of her," Maria says on her way out.

Lauren combs her mother's faded colored hair, waters the flowers, and exchanges the old magazines for the new ones. Her mother tells her she wants to take a walk so Lauren unplugs the IV/drug machines and drapes a second hospital gown over her down-turned shoulders since the single one always opens in the back.

12:21 p.m.

Large gurneys are lined up on either side of the walls of the west wing cancer corridor, and they have to edge the IV around them. Origami birds are affixed to the ceiling above, and she and her mother point out to each other the ones they like: tessellations and kusudama. Her mother moves haltingly, and her breath comes fast. For a fleeting moment, Lauren imagines that this slow-moving person beside her is someone other than her mother. She has to pause to speak. "Dad called last night."

"What'd he say?" Lauren asks.

"He can't believe it — like everyone. No one can believe this happened to me."

Why couldn't it have been him? Lauren thinks, not for the first time. He's the one who drank and smoked; the one whose notion of exercise is to walk from the house to the car.

"Six weeks ago, I was walking five miles on the beach and playing two sets of doubles!" her mother says, breathlessly. Though she'd always kept busy, after the divorce her mother had a rebirth: she played in tennis tournaments, was elevated to a managerial position at her cosmetic sales job, and traveled to all the places Lauren's father had never wanted to go. Lauren's mind flashes back to when her mother drove to New York from Boston, the time Lauren got her heart broken, arriving within hours. Flash. Her mother confidently telling her something better would come along when she

33

missed out on a job she'd wanted. Flash. Her mother cheering her on when she ran the New York Marathon every year. Flash. Her mother completely rebuilding her life in Los Angeles to help Lauren raise the kids.

"You're still strong." Lauren speaks quickly, shutting the memories out of her mind, like a window shade.

"You bet I am." Her mother's voice is void of the uncertainty that plagues Lauren night and day.

1:14 p.m.

The last thing Lauren wants to do when she leaves the hospital is meet a stranger. But a friend told her about a friend's sister from England who has a "killer script". People are always asking her to read scripts, even though she hasn't worked in the movie business for six years, since the twins were born. Mike often says she has to learn to say no, and though she always agrees with him, when it comes to the moment of saying no, she always says yes.

When she gets to her car, Lauren sees that she has a parking ticket. She pulls the envelope from under her windshield wiper, stuffs it into her bag, and curses herself for not paying the hospital parking, a fraction of the cost of the ticket.

A pale thin woman with a shaved head approaches Lauren when she walks into the coffee shop. She is wearing a fake fur-collared sweater, which gives the odd impression that her hair has abandoned her head for her neck.

"Sorry I'm late. My mother is in the hospital." It surprises her how willingly she uses her mother's illness as an excuse.

When they sit down, Lauren asks Jane to tell her about the script. She only catches about two-thirds of what Jane says because of her accent and how quickly she speaks. Lauren is also distracted by her shaved head. She keeps trying to imagine her mother without hair. When she was little, she brushed her mother's hair for hours.

Though the silver roots were her first glimpse at her mother's mortality, she loved to please her mother, and brushed on.

"My mum died seven years ago," Jane says, as if she knew her thoughts. "I still miss her. Tell me about your mother."

Lauren has been cataloguing people's dead mother stories ever since her mother was diagnosed. "It spread outside her ovaries."

"Are you sure you're up for reading this?" Jane flips the script's pages like a deck of cards.

"Sure," Lauren lies. "It'll help distract me."

2:50 p.m.

When Christian gets into the car he throws a flyer at her that says there is no school tomorrow for "teachers' day", whatever that means. What it *actually* means for her: dragging Christian with her to see her mother or not seeing her mother at all.

Lauren ignores the sheet, or rather, his throwing it at her. So much of her interaction with Christian relies on her ignoring things. "How was school?"

"What's *he* doing here?" Christian eyes his brother — whom Lauren picked up first today — with contempt.

"I was at his school, so I got him first," she says, as upbeat as possible.

"When are you working in *my* school again? You're always at *his* school."

Lauren reminds him that she'd been at *his* school the previous week.

"That doesn't count. It was Eve's birthday."

She tells him how the volunteer system works, then says, "Understand?"

No answer.

Lauren turns around. Christian has his iPod on and is looking away.

"Please God make these difficult traits translate into something positive when he's older!"

Christian turns away from the window and looks at her. "Whad'ya say Mom?"

"I love you."

"That's not what you said."

"Oh yes it is."

3:14 p.m.

They're late to Christian's soccer practice. "Now I won't get to play center!" He tosses his gear bag at her before taking off, onto the field.

While Christian is at practice, Lauren drops Ethan across town at his new chess lesson. The instructor is staring at his oversized watch. He is only a boy, certainly not more than twenty-five, and wears wire-rimmed glasses that look like they can barely contain the thickness of the lenses. "You need to get here on time." These are the first words he's spoken to her, face to face.

Ethan adores chess and is already sitting in his place, contemplating a move, so Lauren resists the urge to say something about her mother.

4:04 p.m.

The boy chess instructor looks at his watch when she and Christian hustle through the library door four minutes late.

"Normally my mother helps with driving the kids around but she's in the hospital, so I have to shuttle between both kids' appointments." Lauren writes the boy a check and hands it to him. His hands are fleshy. He folds the check and puts it into the waist pocket of his sweater vest. "She has cancer — my mother."

Without a word, he looks off and opens the door for them to leave.

4:54 p.m.

She forgot the fennel she needs for dinner, so Lauren drives to a small vegetable store near the house. At a red light, she feels herself dozing off. Damn that cat, she thinks. She picks up her phone and calls Mike to keep herself awake.

"I was just going to call you," he says. "I have to go out later tonight. I'll get the kids ready for bed first and then leave, okay?" Lauren lifts the morning's to-go coffee cup, stares with dismay at the dregs. "How are the boys? Your mom?"

"Okay." Suddenly, she wants to hang up. She often becomes mute when there is too much to say. "Ethan liked chess," she manages.

When she hangs up the phone, Christian leans into the front seat. "How come you didn't tell Dad anything about me?"

"Oh, Christian." Lauren can almost feel the line between her eyes deepen.

When they get to the market, Christian shouts, "I'm not going in!" He's turned up his iPod and can't gauge the volume of his own voice.

"Me too, Mom." Ethan re-buckles his seatbelt.

Lauren doesn't have the strength to fight them on it, or maybe she wants to give a win to Christian. She has only the fennel to get, and the car is close enough to the door. Two minutes later when she walks out of the store, plastic bag under arm, a meter maid is standing there looking at her.

"Is this your car?" There's judgment in her voice.

Lauren nearly drops her bag running to look in the car. She can't answer the meter maid until she sees the boys. Did she really just bargain her mother's life for her kids in her mind? She isn't sure, because a minute later when she spots both boys' heads, she is already denying it to herself.

"Did you read the papers this week? Abduction on 6th Street." The meter maid punches Lauren's license plate number into a hand-held computer and hands her the second parking ticket of her day.

"My mother is in the hospital fighting for her life. Have a heart."

The meter maid ignores her. Lauren leaves without waiting for the ticket.

"Christian hit me in the head!" Ethan says at the same time that Christian says, "He knocked my iPod with his foot." Lauren revs the car, holds the wheel tight. It's easy for her to imagine cancer and other diseases feeding on stress. She feels every family argument in her gut; her emotions connect to her stomach like consecutive train stops.

"Ouch!" Ethan cries. "Mom!"

Lauren takes a deep breath and yells "CHRISTIAN!!!!!"

The boys are as silent as sand. Lauren peers at them in the rearview mirror. Her reaction has scared them both. She knows that she's lost; that she will not forgive herself for yelling at them. Growing up, her mother lost her temper at times. She understands that she is passing her rage onto them too, like a family heirloom.

"I'm sorry, guys." She pulls into the driveway. "I'm having a hard time with Nana being in the hospital." Both boys are watching her closely. Christian offers to take in some bags. Ethan shuts the car door for her. She feels like a patient. Like her mother.

"I want to call Nana," Ethan says.

"Let's wait till six, after she's eaten." Lauren doesn't recognize the hollowness of her own voice.

5:01 p.m.

The cat is waiting by the door. She meows in a yelling way. The vet had said she would die within four months. Nine months later, here she is, meowing as loudly as ever.

"Whoever said cats were independent did not know you, Nancy." Lauren tries to force lightness back into the room, like air freshener.

"What's that smell?" Christian looks at her making a face.

"Nancy peed again. My day is complete." After a ten-minute search, Lauren finds a towel reeking of cat piss on the bathroom floor. As she cleans, her movements are slow, weighted.

The cat follows her into the kitchen. Lauren rummages through the fridge while listening to messages. She feeds the cat, who sniffs the food, then walks away. It is the only time the cat ever walks away from her.

Lauren opens a bottle of wine, pours herself a generous glassful, and drinks an uncivilized gulp.

6:11 p.m.

Lauren calls her mother twice, but there is no answer.

7:11 p.m.

"What a day." Mike exhales loudly when he walks through the door. He says hello to the kids and peruses the mail before launching into his diatribe.

Lauren stands at the counter spooning food onto plates, shoulders stooped, half listening to him gripe about selfish rock stars and neurotic co-workers. She feels like a tea kettle with all of the day's emotions boiling, whistle about to blow.

"How's your mom? Did you get a chance to pay her bills?"

Lauren stops moving. "I just realized I lost my first home."

"Jesus, babe, she might be okay." Mike puts an arm around her. "You know, you really should try to be more positive."

Lauren leans into him. "I meant her ovaries, honey. The hysterectomy."

8:00 p.m.

Her mother answers on the first ring.

"Everything okay?"

"Pat died tonight." Her mother is crying. Lauren pictures the bed next to her mother's, empty, except for the stuffed animals. For the first time, she hears the fear in her mother's voice. Though it terrifies Lauren, she consoles her mother with untruths about the differences between their cancers, the stages.

8:05 p.m.

Lauren hangs up the phone and sits down. She feels like nothing in the world will ever be easy again. She can't imagine living, much less laughing without her mother. She has this urge to tell her mother that *I will never laugh again without you.* She hears more shouts from upstairs but the thought of moving only makes her feel heavier. Of course, the cat seizes the opportunity to jump onto her lap. She has to give her credit for her unflagging optimism, just like her namesake. Before kids, she pampered the cat, talked to her like a friend. She used to think it knew when she was in pain. Now she just thinks the cat is narcissistic. Now that she has nothing left to give.

By the time she gets upstairs, the kids and Mike are asleep. She nudges Mike's leg to wake him, drags herself to her bed as she hears him leave for some club — the thought of which makes her more tired. It's all she can do to undress.

12:31 a.m.

It's after midnight when Mike gets home. She hears him check on the boys, run the water, shake out vitamins, gargle, and flush the toilet. She moves towards him when he climbs into the bed, but it isn't her husband, it's Christian. She remembers how she yelled at him earlier and embraces her son tightly.

4:00 a.m.

Lauren wakes with a start. She looks at Christian beside her, sees his pajamas are dry, then goes to check on Ethan. He lies asleep in his space bed. Nancy. Where's Nancy? Wondering only makes her feel more awake. Might as well find her and then try to sleep, she thinks. Lauren switches off the boys' nightlight and tiptoes downstairs, looking around for the cat. She walks to the kitchen, expecting the cat to follow. She makes herself some tea, and when the cat still hasn't come in, she cleans the cat's bowls — the sound of which can summon the cat from the deepest sleep, the furthest corners of the yard. Still no cat.

"Nancy!" Lauren loudly whispers, walking from room to room. She feels herself starting to convulse, with each step, her body caving in on itself, already certain that her cries are going unheard. Lauren walks outside and stares into the darkness. "Nancy, come to Mommy!" She cries over and over and over again, each wail more desperate than the last. "Come to Mommy! Please!"

Christian's Dab Bay

3:29 a.m.

You wake up wet. Again. Pee is everywhere: on your pajamas, three pillows, two covers, and one sheet. It's stupid, the space it covers. In the toilet, it looks so small. Away from the bowl is different, like the humungous puddle you made that time on the ground when your parents had pulled off the highway because you couldn't hold it in all the way to Big Sur. When your teacher, Ms. Beverly, told the class she had visited Big Sur last weekend, you didn't listen to her describing the cliffs and other stuff. You thought of that puddle of pee, big enough to have dirt, rocks, ants, and, best of all, a Hershey's bar wrapper, carried away in it, like a gigantic tidal wave or something.

The soaked pajamas come off. Thinking of Ms. Beverly reminds you of tomorrow. You shiver, and let yourself think about how cold it is, so you don't think about school the next day. The last day of your life, probably.

3:31 a.m.

You walk to your parents' bed, still smelling like pee, and stand until Mom jumps up, sets you down, and tucks you in. This bed is so much more comfortable. Once you thought that wetting the bed was almost worth it to have this feeling — like hot chocolate and socks after skating. Now, you wish you could stop, but then it happens again, and again. The warmth makes you feel sleepy.

4:29 a.m.

The sound of Nancy meowing wakes you. You love Nancy and are worried about her. She's sick, like Nana. "Both my Nancy's are sick." Mom has been saying this a lot, because the cat was named after your grandmother. Nana takes you to the movies and calls you the nicest dessert names, like "sugar cookie," "angel cake," and "pumpkin pie" in a singing kind of voice. Mom walks by whispering for the cat to be quiet. You don't like the way she's talking to Nancy and want to tell her to stop. Nancy is sick. She can't help it.

4:33 a.m.

You lie in bed and picture a robber coming into the room, then throw the covers over your head. The air under here smells like farts so you poke only your nose out, feel for Dad's foot, and fall back to sleep.

6:35 a.m.

The sound of Nancy throwing up wakes you this time. Why do you have to go to school today? For sure, it's going to be the end of your life. Art, music, and P.E. are great, but why do you have to do the things like reading? Who made that rule? Like that Sponge Bob where Patrick magically disappeared whenever he didn't want to do anything? Pretty soon, he was never there. You could say you're sick, but then no soccer. Maybe you could excuse yourself and go to the bathroom again? But you've done that too many times already. Besides, Ms. Beverly said that today was definitely your turn to....Wait. Stop thinking about this — you're supposed to be sleeping. God, are you dumb. You can't even remember what you're not supposed to remember.

7:19 a.m.

"Did Christian sleep in your bed? Did he wet his pants again?" Ethan asks.

It's final. You hate Ethan forever and ever, till eternity.

"Did he?" Dad asks, like it's everybody's business.

You sit awake in bed feeling worse than an hour before, and throw a pillow at Ethan. "Shut-up jerk-face!" Then turn to your father. "Thanks a lot, Dad."

"What'd I do?" Ethan asks.

"What'd I say?" your father says. Sometimes, your family are even stupider than you.

You get up, and walk away. Go to the bathroom. "Small bladder," Mom calls it. This is supposed to make you feel better. It doesn't. There are certain words that mean the same thing as baby. Small is one of them. Tiny, little, and even cute are not words you want to hear used to describe anything about you. Dad calls the penis "weenie". You don't like that either since it rhymes with teeny. You stand and wait for the pee that had no problem coming out last night to come out now. Is some sort of trick someone is playing on you? It's hard to think of your penis without thinking of Ethan. Twins. People sometimes mix the two of you up. If they saw you both naked, they'd see the difference. He may be older by one minute, but you can't help wanting to tell him he has a teeny weenie whenever he mentions your peeing in the bed. So what if he's better at reading.

Dad walks into the bathroom to wash his hands. The sound of the running water finally makes the pee come. As it does, you think of the Cheerios Mom used to place in the toilet when she was teaching you how to go to the potty. "Shoot the Cheerio!" she cheered. She left the bright yellow box next to the toilet. Most of the time, you'd close the toilet, sit down and eat. Once, she caught you eating them and sort of yelled. "I'm going poo!" you shouted back and made a really sad face like those puppies at the pet store near the library. It was the first time you lied to Mom. A little part felt bad, but a bigger part felt good, the way she believed you. It made you feel smart. You did tell Ethan about it later, and, of course, he told Mom, which then led to lie number two, where you told them both you were tricking Ethan. He deserved it, the idiot tattle tale.

Ethan stands beside you peeing. The pees cross each other and make a cool "X" mark in the air. Sometimes Ethan is cool. If only you were identical twins, like that movie where the two girl twins switched places. He could go to school for you today. That would be so excellent.

You laugh and aim for an "I," but your pee sprays the side of the toilet.

"Christian missed the bowl," Mr. Tattle Tale says. You hate Ethan.

Dad doesn't hear him or isn't listening, because he's running the bath. You start to walk out of the bathroom. He's still talking but you're not listening cause you're wondering if maybe you could slip and fall on your pee, so you could miss school.

"Hey, Bongo, did you hear me? I said bath time."

"I took a bath yesterday."

"Yeah, and now it's today." Dad hangs up a towel.

"Why do I have to take a bath every day anyway? Rhys doesn't. Alex doesn't."

"You wet the bed." Mr. Perfect, Mr. I'm-Better-Than-You-twin-brother says walking towards the bath. If he can't go to school for you, what good is he?

"Yeah, well you're just a baby." You knock him out of the way and get in first. Excellent move. You'll get the end near the thing where the water comes out.

"And you're a…"

"Guys, guys," Dad says. "Basta."

When Dad leaves, you hold water in your mouth and spit it at Ethan, like that fountain that time with water coming out of the kid statue's mouth in Texas or Italy or somewhere. You can't remember the name.

"Mom!!" Ethan cries. "Christian's spitting water at me!"

What a baby. He's a dumb baby. There's something about him that makes you want to fight. It's not your fault, he's such a cry baby, tattle tale, dumb jerk.

Mom walks in just as you're launching your next mouthful at him.

"Christian!" she yells. Why is it always you who gets in trouble, and perfect Ethan gets away with everything? Why? A lot of times you think they're working together, which is called something, some big word, but you can't think of the name. You want to tell Mom about how Ethan made fun of you wetting the bed, but you don't want to remind them that you wet the bed. Instead, you stand up to get out of the bath, but not without shoving him first on the way out.

"MOM!" stupid fart yells.

"Christian, what did I say?" she shouts from the other room.

"What'd I do? I'm not even near him!" You hurry out of the bathroom and into your own room. "Geez! This is so unfair! How come he never gets in trouble?"

8:15 a.m.

You listen to music on the way to school because you're still mad at Mom and Ethan and want to let them know, and so you don't have to think about reading. The car smells yucky, like puke and French fries. Today, you're listening to Queen and David Bowie's "Under Pressure." The words are hard to understand, but it sounds like they're talking about you. When you hum, Mom turns and smiles. It'd be so cool to be a musician when you grow up. Either that or do what Dad does, finding new musicians. So, why do you have to do this idiot reading thing today? It's not like that's what you want to do when you grow up.

Usually, it bothers you that Ethan gets dropped off first, but today you don't care, because you'd rather do anything than go to school.

When the car turns onto the street where your school is, you feel sick. Sicker. Your heart is beating faster, like it does when you play soccer. A lot of times, you picture the car swerving off the road and crashing. Today, even that doesn't seem like a bad thing. "It'll be a while before Christian is ready for schoolwork," the doctor would say. The iPod slides around in your sweaty hands. You wipe them on your khakis and turn the volume on your iPod up to nine. There's "the brain" Charlie Burns, who wears suspenders and has the shortest haircut of anyone in the world, walking to school himself. At least you're not him. He has no friends. Zero. You spot Alex and Rhys. Normally, you'd jump out and walk in with them, but today you're practicing being invisible.

Pray, pray, pray for Mom to magically say you don't have to go to school today: Why not take the day off and come with me to visit Nana? Instead, she shouts something really loud. Eve's mother, who's just getting out of the next car, looks over. Great, now the whole world knows you're here. Perfect. You take your ear buds out. "Mom! You don't have to yell. My friends probably heard you."

At first, she looks mad. She looks like she's going to yell, but instead she says, "I'll race you to the door, slow poke."

You break into a sprint and easily beat her, as always. You start to smile until you realize where you are. Prison a.k.a. school a.k.a. the place where you will die today.

8:49 a.m.

The day's schedule is clearly marked on the white chalkboard in thick black letters for all to see. You know what it says, and, on purpose, you look down. Still, it's there — your name next to "Reading," visible out of the sides of your eyes, like you're a lizard. It feels like those words are following you. You hate that white board more than anything else in the entire world. You can see words much better on the blackboard at home.

"Sitting balls, please." Ms. Beverly has everyone sit on a ball seat — her idea to make kids better students, but it doesn't seemed to have helped you. Ms. Beverly is not that much taller than you, and she wears thick glasses and has black hair, you think. All color hair, other than blonde and orange, or whatever that color is that Ginny B. has, looks black to you. Ms. Beverly plays the guitar. You like Ms. Beverly. Of course, today would be the day that she tells the class to focus on the schedule because of some change she said but you didn't listen to. She then lists each thing one by one. This is so unfair. Your sort-of girlfriend Jennifer isn't here, which for today is a good thing, otherwise, she might like Alex more. Alex is a great reader, like Ethan.

"Want a sleepover?" You whisper to Rhys. He smells a little gross, like smoke and trees. Mom says his Dad might get cancer because he smokes. But Nana doesn't smoke and she still got it.

"When?"

"I don't know. Tonight?"

"Whose house?" Rhys is dressed in black, like his parents, although sometimes his father wears weird things like a red and white shirt with boxes on it that looks like a picnic-table cloth and bowling shirts with other people's names on them like "Lenny," and "Drake." Dad says his mother looks like Ozzie somebody with her shaded granny glasses and her thin, dark, straight hair parted in the middle.

"Mine." You lean back.

"I went to yours last time."

You can't sleep over at anyone's house because you might pee the bed. Forget that. That would be the worst. No way. "But, I have this thing at my house that I want to...."

"Christian," Ms. Beverly says. "Since you're our superstar reader today, maybe you should pay attention to today's schedule?"

She said it. Great. Superstar reader? Right. More like super stupid reader. You like that. Super stupid reading. You have to tell your friends that one. Of course, she said nothing to Rhys who was talking too. You've changed your mind. Ms. Beverly is not nice. All teachers are mean, like the one from last year who sent you to the principal for the littlest thing. What if Ms. Beverly and the whole class is part of some big thing against you? That word you don't know.

"Now, because we have Lucy's father coming in at 11:00 to discuss his job as a pastry chef, a few things have shifted to after lunch, including superstar reader time." Ms. Beverly is looking straight at you. At least your reading has been moved until later in the day, closer to the time to go home. Maybe then your friends will forget it easier. Wouldn't it be great if there was an earthquake or something, and you all got to go home early? You picture walls falling down, kids hiding under their desks, the balls bouncing everywhere, like a monster-size popcorn popper. You whisper in Rhys's ear, "It's called super stupid reading. S.R. Wait. I mean S.S…"

"Christian?" Ms. Beverly says.

"What?"

"Excuse me, please?" she corrects you.

"I said excuse me." Did she not hear you answer her? Geez.

"So what are we doing at ten to two?"

You think: play dumb so you sound smart. That's worked before. "Ten o'clock? Aren't we home sleeping?"

Everyone laughs. YES!

"One-fifty is also ten to two." None of this makes any sense. There's nothing worse than words and numbers together. How can one be the same as ten?

Jennifer rushes into the room late. Her hair is in long pigtails, and she's wearing shiny pink pants and a vest that says "Cutie". See, you read that, even if she did tell you what it said the last time she wore it. But, yeah, just then, you definitely read it. Maybe you can read now? Maybe it'll magically happen like that. You wish. Jennifer's mother, holding Jennifer's baby brother in her arms, goes up to Ms. Beverly. For a moment, you're happy to see Jennifer, until you remember the super stupid reading. When her mother leaves, Ms. Beverly says, "Oh dear. Look at the time. We have to move on."

Phew. Got out of that one.

10:19 a.m.

At P.E., Coach Trevor divides the class into two teams for dodgeball. You put on little shirts with no sleeves, whatever they're called. You're on the green team and try to get the ball. Some kids complain, call you a "hog," but everyone knows you're the best player in the class.

Who invented reading, anyway? It's so dumb. Charlie Burns might be good at reading, but look how he stinks at dodgeball, hiding behind a few girls. You missile the ball at him Z-Z-Z-ONK — knocking him out of the game. Not only does he fall down, but he starts to cry. What a baby. Good. Maybe your friends will remember Charlie Burns crying today more than whatever happens later.

11:00 a.m.

Lucy's father is talking about bread or something. Bo-ring. Plus, the room smells like envelopes. You can't believe it, Charlie's taking notes! Nudge Rhys and nod at Charlie. Rhys nudges Simon and Simon nudges Flynn. Pretty soon, a lot of you are laughing at Charlie. Part of you feels bad, but another part feels happy, because it helps you not think of the S.S.R. You picture a boat being held captive. "The S.S.R. has been seized by pirates. Destroy!!" Ca-pow, make little explosion sounds and spear a small pink eraser with a pen. "You're going down." The eraser topples to the floor — next to Ms. Beverly's shoe. She picks it up, places it on the desk, puts a finger to her lips, and points to Lucy's father.

Later, Lucy's father passes out two cinnamon cookies to each kid in the class with their initials on them. At least one good thing came out of his boring talk. You get a "C" and an "L". Your "C" cookie looks a little smaller than some of the other cookies; Charlie's "C" is much bigger. You're about to say something when Alex says Paul Utner's cookies spell "P.U.". Isabella Kendrick's "I.K." is funny too. Why can't reading be this simple? Just initials.

"No eating cookies until after lunch time," Ms. Beverly warns the class. You really don't like Ms. Beverly anymore, maybe for the rest of your life.

12:21 p.m.

Mom packed you the worst lunch ever: peanut butter on some weird bread with little black bug-like things on it, an apple that has a bruise (WORMS!!) that you shoot across the room — three points! — into the trash, mozzarella sticks that are okay, but there's only two, and you finish them in a second, and a yogurt that has a different label than usual, so another three-pointer that explodes on impact, and deserves one more point. Rhys' has popcorn, and Jennifer has dinosaur chicken, which, luckily, she shares with you. At least you have the cookies from Lucy's father to eat. You drink juice and look over at Charlie Burns, sitting alone, reading while he eats this disgusting-looking sandwich with green stuff in it. Looking at Charlie reminds you that after lunch it'll be time for the stupid reading. Suddenly, you don't feel hungry anymore. You look down at the cookies. Half of the "C" is eaten, and there's still the "L" cookie to eat.

"Charlie's reading," you say. "His cookies should have been I.D., for idiot."

Someone spits a straw wrapper at Charlie. Then another. But Charlie looks like there's nothing in the world that would make him look up. You remember how someone from school was mean to Ethan. That's what happens if you read too much.

Walking back to class, you feel as heavy as a hill of cows. Now, everyone is forming a circle. You look at the door and wish your mom was there. You walk over to Ms. Beverly. "I think I'm sick."

"Christian, don't worry. You're fine. If you still feel sick afterwards, I'll call your mother. Okay?"

Don't answer. Try not to look at Jennifer and Rhys. The room looks so different from up here, like a whole other school. You pretend it's a whole other school; one where no one will care about how stupid you are.

"Quiet, please," Ms. Beverly says. "Eyes on Christian. Okay, Christian."

Holding your breath, slowly, you open the book. The letters seem like they're flying around the page. The pictures, you sort of think/shout to yourself. Maybe they'll help. Ms. Beverly said before there were words, cavemen used to draw pictures. Why did someone have to invent words anyway? You hate that person more than anyone in the whole world. In the book, there is a picture of an elephant carrying a towel, a ball, and a lunchbox.

"Christian," Ms. Beverly says. Of course, stopping to check out the pictures automatically makes you seem dumb cause it slows you down. Bad start, stupid.

"Okay, okay." Slowly, you start to read. "Pat is go-ing to the be-a-k. I mean beach," you quickly correct yourself. Looking up, you lose your place. "Pat-is-go...Oh, I read that part already," you laugh. Silence. Why is everyone so serious? You're sweating. "It's a little too hot in here. Maybe from the cookies." Everyone looks at you like you just said something stupid, which you did, even though you meant it to be funny.

"I think it's okay. Take your time. Start with He."

"It's really hot." Ms. Beverly is shaking her head. Staring at the page for a while, you realize you've forgotten what word you were on. "Where was I?"

"Right here." She points to the word in the book. There's a whistle from out on the field. If only you could snap your fingers and be out there.

"Thank you." Maybe you'll get some extra points saying that. "He is ta-king a ball, a t-," you stumble.

"Sound it out, Christian."

"T-o." Just then, you remember the towel picture. "Towel." You get a little excited, until you see what comes next. "And his l-oo," you glance up at Ms. Beverly and block out the others faces all around her. "I can't..."

"Of course you can. The 'u' is soft. 'Lu...'."

"Lunch?" You guess. How could you have forgotten the picture? If only you could be home in bed having this bad dream. Soon, you'll wake up and go to Mom and Dad's bed.

"Yes!"

When you glance up, you see Eve whispering to Charlie. Charlie stares down at the carpet, like he doesn't want to embarrass you. Why did you treat Charlie bad? If you make it through this, you are going to be nicer to him for the rest of your life, or at least until Christmas.

"Please continue." Ms. Beverly claps her hands twice.

You turn the page and see the elephant in the car. "The car is no."

"Is it "no" or "on"?"

"I can't do this." You smell carpet and food mixed together.

"Of course you can. "No" or "on?""

"On," you answer and read it faster. "The-car-is-on. At-the-beach-Pat-meets-his-fr-fr-i-I-mean-friend-Bob. Bob-says-he-llo-to-Pat." You shift in your feet but feel a little better. That last page went okay. Going faster works. You turn the page and continue, "Bob-lo-ook-at-the...

"Looks," Ms. Beverly corrects you.

"Looks," you say. "At-the-sky.-There-is-no-sun.-This-is-a-dab-bay...."

Someone laughs. You look up and see one kid nudges another. Another is covering his mouth to stop from laughing. At least your friends are looking down or away, as is Charlie Burns. Why are all books white? It feels like your whole life is a trick against you.

Ms. Beverly walks over. "You are doing great, Christian. Read that last line one more time slowly, and then you're done."

It feels like you've been up here for your whole life. "I can't...."

"One word at a time."

"I can't." Maybe a dinosaur or an elephant will walk in the room and flatten her. Now. Now. Now. Now. Now.

Ms. Beverly sits next down and puts a finger on each word. Slowly, you read them. "This-is-a-bad-day-for-the-beach." Bad day, idiot! Unbelievable. Dab bay? God, are you dumb! Dumb! Dumb! Dumb! At least you know that much. It's dumb, not bum, but you're that too, aren't you?

Ms. Beverly puts her arm around your shoulder and says, "I'm very pleased, Christian. Okay, you can sit." Grown-ups are so bad at lying.

You walk towards the back of the reading circle and wonder about Ethan's school. If only they didn't have all that homework. Tests too, more than this school. At least everyone there doesn't know that there's something wrong with you. Or maybe you could ask about moving to another city, like Susan Hoffman did last year. Ms. Beverly is writing in red ink. She's going to tell your parents that you are the only kid in class who can't read.

1:58 p.m.

Life is over. You barely pay attention for the rest of the day. It feels like you're in a giant fish bowl. Kids are staring too. If only you could be glad that it's done, but it was so bad that it's impossible to be happy. You change your mind about Ethan's school. You'll look even dumber next to Ethan, which is why Mom and Dad put you in different schools, even though they don't say that. "We want you to have your own I-dents," they said. I-dents is not the word, but since your life just ended, all words feel wrong to you. Sometimes you think of Ethan as a thief. While you both slept inside Mom, he stole some of your brains. You imagine trading things with each other, like baseball cards. "I'll give you 'good at math' and 'great at reading' for 'fantastic at sports' and 'an ear for music'." Since he was born a minute earlier, he must have taken all the smart cards. Which is definitely why you should hit him.

Though you can't read the clock, you pray for it to move faster, for the bell to ring.

2:50 p.m.

In the car, you throw a flyer at Mom. "No school tomorrow?" she says. "Again?" At least your friends will have a day to forget about what an awful reader you are. You want to tell Mom about what happened but can't because your jerk brother is in the car. "How was school?" Mom asks. It's all you can do to not cry. Isn't it her job to protect you? How could she have let it happen?

"What's he doing here?" You wish you could push that jerk brother who stole half your brains out of the car so he falls out onto the street and gets hit by a bus or a truck.

"I was at his school, so I got him first." There it is: Mom loves Ethan more. Why not? He's smarter.

"When are you working in my school again? You're always at his school." If Mom had come to your school more, maybe you'd be a better reader.

"I was just at your school last week. Remember?"

Pick up the iPod, put the buds in both ears and rewind to "Under Pressure" again. Mom is saying something. "Difficult:" you heard that word loud, like that special cone-thing the gym coach uses to talk into.

"Whad'ya say, Mom?"

"I love you."

"That's not what you said."

"Yes it is."

Turn the volume up and move towards the window. This is, by far, the worst day ever. Even your mom is lying. You remember all your little lies and think, *if she's lying to me, I'm definitely going to keep lying to her.*

3:14 p.m.

You arrive late to practice and don't get to be a forward. The whole game, the words "Dab Bay" flash over and over in your mind, as if someone is hammering them in there. They're so simple. How did you get them mixed up?

Back in the car, alone with Mom, you want to tell her about what happened today. "Mom?"

"Yeah?"

"Hmm?"

"Um, Mom?" Tell her. Maybe she can help make it better.

"Uh-huh?"

"Um…"

"What is it babe?"

"Um...." What if she talks to your teacher? What if they do take you out of school, or worse, hold you back while all your friends move up? You know you said you wanted to leave school, but then what? And where would they put you? What if they gave more homework or something? Or what if she takes you to the doctor and they say you need an operation?!

"Sweetie?"

"Oh, nothing."

4:04 p.m.

The guy teaching Ethan chess is mean to Mom. You can't believe Ethan would choose to play chess with this meanie instead of soccer. Crazy. There are a few trophies in a case, and you walk over to them. Next to each trophy is a picture of a kid and the weird-o teacher. Next to the biggest trophy is a picture of Charlie Burns smiling so big that you almost don't recognize him. You've never seen him smile like this at school. Never ever. You remember what you did to him today and think how you deserved to have this BAD DAY.

4:54 p.m.

When Mom stops at the store, you throw a balled-up piece of cardboard at Ethan to catch. He's not such a bad brother mostly. He thinks you meant to be mean, so he hits you. Just then, you notice her: the police!! Your heart is jumping like there's someone on a pogo stick inside your chest. What if something happened to Mom?!! You start to cry. Ethan laughs. He must think you're kidding. You get mad at him laughing and hit him in the head, just as Mom opens the door. You are so happy to see her! You were about to run.

"Christian hit me in the head!" Baby Ethan is crying to Mom.

"No fair! He hit me first!"

Mom says nothing and drives away from the police lady. You're about to ask her about this, but Ethan kicks you, so of course you have to get him back. You smash into him and he yells, "Ouch! Mom!"

"CHRISTIAN!" Mom yells so loud you forget that she didn't say Ethan's name. Now you feel really scared. What would you do without her? It's even worse when she apologizes and mentions Nana. That stupid reading today made you totally forgot about Nana. This is awful. Even when you try to be good, you are really bad.

5:01 p.m.

Nancy the cat peed somewhere. You pet her neck a lot of times because Mom is frustrated with her. Afterwards, you construct a Lego space station with great portals and take these little flags from one of Ethan's boring games to represent each of the nine planets.

When you show Mom, she says over and over how creative you are. You can tell she feels bad about yelling.

6:11 p.m.

You think how your Nana needs to be all better so your Mom will be happy again, so she can help you get better at reading. But all that seems impossible.

7:11 p.m.

When Dad comes home, he and Mom talk all serious-like. What if they got divided, or whatever that word is that happens when parents don't live together. Would one take Ethan and one take you or would you both go together? You decide Mom would definitely take Ethan because she likes to read, too. You get really sad thinking of not living with Mom. Maybe if you try realllllllly hard to be nice to Ethan — and Charlie too — maybe you can still live with Mom?

8:00 p.m.

Mom is downstairs on the phone when Dad is getting you ready for bed. You know she's talking to Nana 'cause she sounds different. Dad fills the bath and wants you to get in, but all you want to do is to see Mom. When you finally do get in, it's too cold. If only you could shoot this day away with a laser beam.

"I want Mommy to get me out of the bath." You sink into the water.

"Honey!" Dad shouts. "Are you almost done?"

8:05 p.m.

You are really scared. Mom is not coming up. Why are all these bad things happening? You used to be able to memorize picture books, but now there are just too many words on the page. What if something is wrong with you? Really wrong. Or maybe all of this bad is happening because you were mean to Charlie today? Be nicer or else you're going to have another dab bay, dab bay, dab bay. You make yourself remember those words because you were bad to Charlie, who's never been mean his whole entire life.

You put some strawberry toothpaste on Ethan's planet-earth-shaped toothbrush. then on your soccer ball one. Still, Mom is not upstairs.

"When's Mom coming up?"

"Soon." He looks at his watch.

"But when?"

"Really soon."

"Can I go get her?" You start walking towards the stairs.

"No."

"But, I…"

"Hey, buddy, stop."

You keep walking.

"Christian, if you go down those stairs, you're not playing soccer this weekend." You remember about trying to be better and stop.

While getting in bed, you decide to ask Charlie for a play date. Mom can call. Ethan can play with him while you watch, or something.

12:31 a.m.

You have a bad dream where these giant cookies with letters on them are knocking you around the soccer field, especially the "C" letter. At first you think it's Charlie's cookie, but then you realize that your name begins with a "C" too. You jump out of bed and walk into Mom and Dad's room. As you turn over to go back to sleep, you notice you didn't wet the bed. You're so excited, you don't fall right back to sleep.

4:00 a.m.

No school tomorrow. Or is it today? Already it's a good day, you think as you write the words "good day" in the black air above you.

Saving Gracie

It was fatal to go downstairs. She would be sucked into the machine, twirled around with all the gunge and spat out two hours later, her best energy gone. Tom would be sitting, legs curled up, sipping tea in the corner, oblivious to everything going on around him. The children would huddle round demanding to be fed, and the table, the heartland of the family, would menace her until she sorted through its motley piles: library books, school letters, bills, bits of toys, lego, and junk mail which thudded on the mat throughout the day, promising pizzas with extra toppings and free delivery, and little men who could come and do for her, go for her.

Inside her, an antique farmhouse table scrubbed clean with a ceramic bowl delicately filled with carefully selected fruit, struggled to break free.

"Have you fed the kids yet?" she asked Tom.

"No, but I watered them."

"Thanks."

All pretence of affection had long since gone. Now she felt her husband with the instinct of a barn owl. He held few surprises for her.

After breakfast the children were packed off upstairs, their little arms crossed and bulging with books, bricks, bits of train and Barbie doll legs. "You have rooms," she said, "put things away."

She heard their chatter retreating up the stairs, a fading cacophony of small voices united in opposition. Then she turned her glare on Tom.

"Are you going to watch me work all day? I don't know how you have the stomach for it."

She would never understand how some men could happily sit by and be serviced by these inferior beings who occupied dark, shadowy, parallel worlds where all the trivialities of life were dispensed with.

Tom glared back. He had just reached page two hundred and thirty-nine of Jospeh Campbell's 'The Masks of God'. Alexander, invading Persia, had issued instructions that no sacred shrine should be damaged... You could kill the poor bastards but leave their gods alone... And now she was talking about cleaning toilets, Tesco's, taking the bloody dog for a walk. "Doesn't get done by itself, you know," she was saying in that annoying way as she took off the rubber gloves again.

"I'm doing things all the time," he said, wiping his eyes and scratching his head, as if to take him from one reality to another.

"I noticed."

"Oh, Gracie is the only one who does anything round here. Don't we all know it GRACE," he said, clearly enunciating her name.

She knew the Saturday row was underway yet was powerless to stop it.

"I do more in the first ten minutes I'm up than you do all day," she said.

And then, of course, he was up. The mention of work always made him head for the nearest door.

"I have a few things to do. Have to go out for a bit."

"More like a hit," she scoffed.

Now he would mention her family and how they were all either mad or evil or both. She was having the same row with the same words. They both knew their parts so well, even the body movements, as if it had been choreographed. Only now there were children who knew the parts as well as them. Whose hungry little bodies needed to be fed. Whose hungry little minds listened at doorways, making mental notes to be buried deep in the unconscious and unearthed years later by skilful therapy, where the mention of the word mother would make them burst into tears.

"You invent it all," said Tom, as per usual. "It's so fucking trivial." And he started to sing an O.T.T. version of 'When I fall in love'.

"You didn't fall in love, Tom. You fell in hate."

The shouting began. The pointing of fingers, the threats, the faces contorted by resentment and frustration.

"Don't forget your blood pressure," he sneered as he left the room.

She felt the blood pounding in her head. The familiar sensation of fluttering in her chest and the beads of sweat on her forehead and between her breasts. She stooped to pick up a Barbie doll shoe, deep pink and perfect, and stared at it for the longest time.

Somewhere in another life, hundreds of years ago, she had been a child. She had looked at the world as if it was a stage set; the buildings were vast and interchangeable, the people came and went saying their lines, dogs pissed against lamp posts, the moon, new and crescent-shaped, peeped from behind police stations, and everything was deep green and bright blue.

Tom would never understand her. How, when the house was empty, she went back into herself. She put on loud music and washed down the floorboards and shook cushions and placed them neatly on the sofas. Everything in its place. How she stool at the sitting room door and looked back into the room as if she was looking at a painting.

✱

"Your blood pressure is very high", the doctor said, his face grim. "There's no point in not telling you. If you go on like this you could have a stroke. You know the risks. You must take the treatment. Think of your children."

She was losing the battle. For two years, since hearing about the blood pressure, she had done everything to bring it down so she wouldn't have to take the medication. "You'll be on it for the rest of your life," the GP had said on that first occasion, after all the investigations. "I'm sorry. It's the way the cookie crumbles." And she had gone home without a prescription to months of splitting headaches and bad nights.

And now he had his hand on the pad.

"It's in your family, Mrs Hawthorne," he was saying. "You have to accept it. When things get less stressful for you it will probably go down a little." And then, as she was leaving the surgery, he added, "Try to do less. You can't be all things to everyone. Let others do the fetching and carrying."

❁

The women splashed around the warm blue pool. A dozen women of assorted shapes and sizes, some looking like huge dolphins on the surface of the water with their tight swim caps.

"Hold hands and run round in a circle," said the instructor. The music pumped out Madonna, Prince, Adele. They felt silly. They were holding hands like children and going round in circles, the warm water whooshing between their thighs. The instructor told them to change direction; the current had built up against them and it was hard to push against the water. They laughed. A little French woman stood at one end of the pool refusing to join in. She was being childish. At first she had been making some kind of statement, doing her own little dance, but now the gesture had worn thin and it was too late to join in.

A woman, who she later found out was in her mid-forties, got out of the pool. She was an American who had never married or had children. She had the same unused body as a young woman. Life had made little impression on it. Her face, too, looked unlived in. Perhaps unloved in. It had none of the usual battle marks on it.

None of the scowls left from years of waiting for the sound of a key turning in the door. Or it's your turn to put the kids to bed, read the story, do the shopping. Your turn. There was something almost ugly, she thought, about this blatant lack of use of life. Later conversations revealed that Sherry worked in the city. She was in IT. She wore neat, dark suits and carried a poncey briefcase, noticed on signing in. She moaned about the men she worked with. "I have no desire to be in a man's world," Gracie had said. "I have to work," Sherry told her coldly. "What are the alternatives?"

The other women's bodies looked used and battered compared to Sherry's. Their bellies drooped and hung from childbirth. their breasts sagged from feeding. They looked like empty pods which had shed their peas. Their faces had expressions which each understood. A joke would be quipped and laughter would break out. They understood each other well.

They knew all about men, children, working, cleaning, cooking, shopping. They knew about hot flushes, panic attacks, loaded bags and checkouts, and the desire to dump everything and run and hide. They knew about work surfaces, stacks of plates, dirty saucepans and cupboards full of pasta, ragu, canned chickpeas and chopped tomatoes. And they knew about washing machines and washing liquid and washing machine men and having to stay in between nine and one. "I was bloody waiting for hours," said Avril, "then the jerk doesn't bloody turn up." "Me too," said Annie, "I was waiting for hours for this guy to come from the council to do the cat fleas. I was in for the flea man, the gas man and the telly man. Unfortunately, when the man-man came I was out!" And they knew about working and having to arrange for someone else to pick-up the children and having to obey two masters and the voice in their heads that retreated so far in it could hardly be heard until one day it surfaced as a scream.

She had come to a health spa for the week. Each morning she went down to the pool to start the day with water aerobics. Then there would be the treatments; acupuncture, massage, reflexology, mud baths, aromatherapy... There was a conveyor belt feel to it. The acupuncturist called three names and took them in to lie side by side separated by thin curtains through which you could hear everything, so nobody said anything. Then she grabbed a packet of disposable needles and proceeded with all the tact and sensitivity of a vet. Arthritis, bam, bam; diabetes, bam, bam; blood pressure, bam, bam. Bam, bam, bam; sometimes the odd question, but mercifully no cooking, no cleaning, no lists.

While waiting in the treatment areas she picked up fragments of conversations. "So I told him, I did. 'You can have the children. I'll get my own place.'" "I agreed to do the cleaning on his place and cook the meals if he would pay the mortgage on mine..." "If you didn't get on with your mother, you feel things more on your left side..." "I never knew the old sod. He went back to Australia when I was a baby and, just when I get it together to go and see him, after years of looking for him, he bloody dies..."

Every evening something very small and warm was put beside a cold salad, followed by an apple or an orange and a cup of lukewarm herb tea. After three days she began to feel like she would murder for a cup of tea. After four, a group of them were sneaking into a nearby town for carrot cake in tearooms. The rest of the time she plodded about in her towelling dressing gown and mules. She began to feel lighter and her skin began to shine, and the word toast took on a whole new meaning and was something to be valued.

She took part in a therapy group. The therapist said it was their job to take responsibility for their own lives. It was no use blaming anyone. Today was the day they were going to change. A teacher said they should learn from their experiences. The scientist said they should analyse them. The writer said they should write them down, and the journalist said they should sell them. She said "I'm sick of being told I chose my parents". Everyone laughed and the writer said write that down, but the legal secretary said don't sign anything.

Slowly the resentment began to melt away and now, when she thought about Tom, the brick in her hand began to fade. A nurse told her her blood pressure was well down, "but it will go up again as soon as you go home" she laughed. "You mark my words. It always does."

One evening, when she was dozing after supper, she dreamt she was at a lecture on Life Choices. A man stood on a darkened stage in a spotlight. He said he was there to tell them the meaning of life. Pick a card, he said. Any one. But choose carefully, he said, inviting people up onto the stage. Pick wisely. After a few years you may want to change your life. But it's not easy. You will be older. There will be casualties. You will not have the same enthusiasms or energy with which to embrace your new life. She got up and nervously edged her way to the stage. She was just about to read what was written on the card he handed her when she woke up. Someone was gently saying her name, "Grace, Grace", like a nurse calling her back after an operation. "Grace, your husband is on the phone."

It was almost time to go home. She was surprised at how little she had thought of Tom. She'd never been away from the children for more than an evening, it had never felt right to her. "They won't want to know you in a few years," Liz, her best friend was always saying. "You'll have to let them go soon enough. Start making a life for yourself - or it will only bring you grief." Liz was one of the few people Gracie allowed to tell her anything about the children. Liz had found one of her two teenage sons dead from an overdose a few years back, just before Christmas. But seeing how she grieved for her son had only made Gracie pull the circle in even tighter, even more afraid than usual - afraid that the shadow over her friend's life was somehow touching hers.

Yes, Gracie had surprised herself how easily she had slipped into being away. For a whole week she was prodded, pampered, powdered and passed tenderly from arm to arm, wrapped in a clean white towel, like a baby. Then she went home.

On the last morning she said a quick farewell to her new friends. She felt the spirit of the week leaving her body like air from a pin cushion, and putting on her clothes, which she had hardly worn all week, reminded her of her old self - the forty-five year old woman who had come here a week earlier, worn out and sick - and she felt the depression rise from her stomach where it so often lived with her flagging self-esteem.

When she got home the children crowded round her excitedly at the door. But Amy, the youngest, held back and did not welcome her. She could smell bleach, and as she made her way to the kitchen, she found Tom with a mop in his hand and a bucket. His hair was standing up and he looked pathetic. He'd made an enormous last-minute effort to make the place look good for her and still it looked terrible. He put the kettle on and the children made toast. But after the fresh home-baked wholewheat bread at the health farm, the packaged sliced bread looked gross, and after the simple whiteness of the spa with its potted ferns, her place looked shabby. Puck smelled bad and whimpered round her feet, vying with the children for attention. Gracie said she wouldn't be a minute and went up to her room at the top of the house. The children tried to follow but Tom held them back.

Gracie looked around her bedroom and started to cry. She did not feel ready for it, ready to go back into her life, back to all the responsibility, all the work. For the first time since she was a child, she had been taken care of, had been allowed to be vulnerable. But then she heard little Amy crying "Mummy, Mummy". Looking over the London rooftops, she dried her eyes. It was a mild spring day and the trees at the bottom of the garden were in blossom. Beyond the garden, Papos, their Greek neighbour, was hard at work in his garage, which he used for carpentry. She changed into some leggings and went into the bathroom to wash her face and comb her hair. Amy came in holding a piece of paper. "Mummy," she said, "while you were away I did this for you. I missed you, Mummy." Grace pulled the child towards her and burying her nose deep in Amy's neck, smelled her little girl.

After All This Time

Have you noticed how on cold but crisp autumn mornings if you stare at the low sun and scrunch-up your eyes you can make it look as if there is a mist laying low over the land? Yet if it is a truly misty start to the day, no matter how wide you open your eyes, the mist never goes away. Why is that? Surely logic would suggest taking an opposite action should generate an opposite reaction. Isn't that Einstein? Or a case of 'some you lose, and some you lose'? I don't know. It just strikes me as odd, imbalanced, out of whack. But then lots of things do, I suppose, if you take the time and trouble to think about them. Having said that - and have you noticed how, as soon as you say one thing, another immediately pops into your head, often to baldly contradict what you had previously thought as if there is a part of you determined to undermine yourself, to always dispute and ridicule, to disprove what you say and think and believe so that you don't actually know what's right any more? Anyway, having said all that about taking the time and trouble etcetera, most people don't have any, do they? Time, I mean, not trouble. Certainly not enough sloshing around for them to be squinting up at the sky. They've got more important things to do, deadlines to meet, trains to catch, mouths to feed, bucks to earn, clothes to buy, drinks to drink, dogs to walk... And not doing things takes time because we have to think about those too, decide *not* to do them, work out avoidance strategies or alternatives. "If it's not one thing it's another" as my old grandmother said. Or may have said. An approximation at least. Not that she has to worry about whether or not there is a morning mist any more, nor the chasing of buses or boiling of potatoes. Unless there's an afterlife and it looks very much like this one. Which would seem a cruel twist, wouldn't it? I mean, "out of the frying pan and into the fire". That could have been another one of hers, couldn't it? If you'd known her you would be able to make your own judgement; but as you didn't, you'll just have to take my word for it. But an afterlife like this one? And what would come after that? Where would it end? We could be worrying about some kind of heaven or hell scenario without realising that we were already living in perpetual purgatory. Some joke that would be. And I wonder what might be different, one world to the next, if anything. Like that thing about mist and eyes. Would there be a world where, when you *did* open your eyes wide, the mist would actually disappear? Or one where there was no Einstein, or the rules of the universe were altered in some way, or the number twenty-four bus always ran on time? You might want to argue at least one of those is too fanciful. But I *do* have the time, just at the minute. Well, for much longer than a minute, obviously. The opportunity to contemplate things because I have no cakes to bake or trains to catch. I'd like to take the credit for being in such an enviable position, I really would. And I may do yet; you know, find a way to harvest the kudos for my situation, my freedom. It seems only right and proper that I should; entirely logical in fact. Why should Benson take any of the credit? All he did was to fire me; *I* was the one who got into the position where I could be fired. Doesn't that make it all my own doing? Doesn't that make Benson something of a puppet of mine, playing the part I had assigned him, merely executing his role based on the situation in which I had placed him? One might even say 'lovingly crafted' for him. Not that I loved him, of course. Not in any incarnation of the word. He was a little man in all senses: stature, philosophy, fellow-feeling, intelligence, imagination. Had he been born many years earlier I'm sure he would have been a pen-pusher. Literally. And perhaps he had been in one of his previous purgatorial lives. It would have been fitting; a part he hadn't even needed to audition for. There are lots of people like that, aren't there? Those who seem to perfectly fit the niche they occupy, round peg etcetera. But surely that can't occur simply by luck. "Oh, here's a hole and it fits me perfectly!" Surely people have to whittle away - either at the hole or at themselves - to become even remotely comfortable. Which is something I have never found myself needing to do, hence there was still surprise in that final confrontation with Benson when he confessed he had to "let me go"; which, to be honest, sounded like a rather generous and most un-Benson-like thing to do. To be let go, to be freed. If you think about it, that's almost beatific, god-like. Which certainly isn't Benson, and therefore all the credit must be mine. Surely. But time - which is the ultimate gift of freedom, isn't it? - can be a tricky bugger. It's as if someone might turn round out of the blue and give you a lifetime's supply of your favourite sweets or cakes. I mean, I like a chocolate eclair as much as the next man, but if you had a never-ending supply of the blood things, well... You'd go off them wouldn't you? They'd cease to be your secret little treat and become something else; mundane, normal. They'd go from special to not-special, just like that. And freedom and time is a little bit like that. Now I have a fridge full of time and I don't know what to do with it. Remember those weekends that were magical, or that short holiday you took to Belgium or wherever? How much were they elevated from the mundane because you had to steal time in order to make them happen? 'Steal'. That's my word. You'd try and eke out as much as you could from every last hour or minute to make the most of things; you'd cram in one more museum or garden or ancient monument not because you could but because you had too. Because time demanded it of you. "Fill me up!" it begged; "Use me, use me!". And you did, and it was great - maybe not at the time, but looking back later when you could, utilising smaller pockets of time in remembering the larger ones. Sitting on the sofa drinking coffee after dinner: "Remember that weekend we had in Tuscany...". It's as if the experience has become doubly special: special at the time, and then special again in its recall. Like the payback on an investment - and one that keeps giving. But now, in my post-Benson world, there is no special time because I have it all. No looking forward to weekends because they mean I won't be working; Saturday and Sunday might just as well be relabelled Monday for all the difference they make to me. Indeed, why not go the whole hog and call every day Monday or Wednesday (not that I ever liked the word 'Wednesday', you understand). Not one minute is outstanding - at least in the sense of 'time', if I may be tantalisingly philosophical. Occasionally there are incidents which trespass on the memorable; there will always be those. But now they exist outside the framework that time - in terms of Monday to Friday, the weekend, the working week, holiday time, half-term, Christmas and so forth - used to overlay on those self-same moments. It is as if *what* I do has become detached from *when* I do it; the symbiotic relationship has been broken. Is that liberating? George thinks it is - though essentially because a) George is jealous, and b) George doesn't know what he's talking about. I've tried to explain it to him, this theory of mine. Perhaps the location of those conversations - the ex-Lounge Bar of 'The Frog and Parrot' - isn't conducive to serious discussion; there's always the background hum of other voices, and from the archway into the Public Bar, the sounds of music or shouts from darts' players when one of them manages to fluke a good shot. Once upon a time 'The Frog and Parrot' was the place to play darts; it had a reputation, won the local league three years on the spin. But then one of the star players moved away from the town and a second switched allegiance to another pub after an argument over a pint of Guinness. It was all downhill after that. When the new landlords Bruce and Shiela (sounds like an Aussie double-act!) arrived a couple or three years ago, they weren't keen on darts, wanted to promote a different atmosphere, talked about the place being "a gastro pub" - which it isn't, by the way. So the darts suffered, the team got relegated or something, then suddenly the matches stopped altogether. There are still a few die-hards who play friendlies of an evening - hence the shouting - but that's about it. George and I chance our arms very occasionally, the odd lunchtime maybe. If I was generous I'd say we were average at best - though all that really matters is that I beat him more than he beats me. Anyway, George struggled to understand my philosophy about time. He couldn't get beyond thinking me a "lucky bugger" because I didn't have to face up to Benson every day. "You can be as jealous as you like," I told him, "but it's not as much plain sailing as you think." He ignored that and often regaled me with what seemed a never-ending list of all the things he would do if he had all the time in the world. Much of it revolved around his precious allotment and when he would plant potatoes and harvest carrots and such like. Most of the rest was typically George; just pie-in-the-sky ideas about going off to the places he'd always wanted to see. However, in the first instance George wasn't the romantic traveller-type he imagined himself to be; and in the second, he simply didn't have the money. He may not have been on the same page as me in terms of freedom from the tyranny of time - if that's what it was - but when it came to the lack of adequate funds we were like peas in a pod. Don't you think I'd be off galavanting about the place if I had a few more zeros on the end of my bank balance? Too right! Under those circumstances I daresay that I'd need to modify my philosophy about time somewhat - which in and of itself begs a different question doesn't it, the relationship between money and time? Actually between money and most things. Money can't buy you happiness? Well, I'd have a bloody good try! "Where would you go?" George asked me one day once he'd finished his own list and confessed to wanting to boogie with Balinese dancing girls and the like. Faced with that question most people would either be like rabbits in headlights or just come up with the few places they already knew and liked. My own approach is much more logical. First I'd rule out the places I wouldn't want to touch, like Africa and the Middle East. And probably a fair chunk of the Far East too. There could also be a big lump of what used to lie behind the Iron Curtain that would score poorly when filtering for an engaging travelling itinerary. Then I'd focus on what was left - which may or may not include South America, depending on the mood I was in. After that the key is not in immediately narrowing down the geography even further (that's a schoolboy error!) but rather to consider *how* you'd want to travel; no point going somewhere and then finding out how you have to get about the place makes you miserable, is there? In my case I wouldn't want to drive. I hate driving. For a couple of years Benson had me on the road all the time; thousands of bloody miles, up and down, everywhere you went looking the same. It was an existence filled with motorways and service stations. I used to see those bloody blue motorway signs in my sleep. So no driving - *unless* I was being driven. In a nice coach; something small and exclusive. But better than that would be, in preferential order, a) trains, and b) boats. Always loved a train, and my soft spot for boats comes, I suppose, from the fact that my Old Man was in the Merchant Navy. Now he *did* go all over the place, including those countries you wouldn't see me dead in. Oh, when you're a kid stories about Kenya and Malaysia and such like are all very well and good - romantic even - but once you've grown up and have a sense of the world, it's like, *really*? Not that I'd cruise in the kinds of rust buckets he used to sail in. Always fancied one of those elegant ships going up and down the Rhine or the Danube, or something more substantial for the Norwegian fjords or whale-watching off the coast of Alaska. See what I mean about needing to focus on how you'd want to travel? It helps define your choices. Not that I shared any of that with George, of course; I doubt he would have understood that logic either. So I just gave him what he expected to hear, named a few European capitals and that was it. I doubt he was really interested anyway. I mean, not *really* interested. Would my Old Man have been disappointed given his background? Seen a lack of ambition in my travel choices? At least I was making a choice, however theoretical; he just went where he was told, subservient to where the ship needed to be. He was a fitter of some kind - which probably meant a lackey with a big spanner. Used to talk to me about various bits of kit he'd worked on, but that was a very occasional interaction. Perhaps he felt he had to try and fill my head with stories when he came home every two or three months. He'd be around for a few weeks working like a regular nine-to-five guy in the dockyard, then all of a sudden he'd not be there, away again, and I'd not see him for ages. Often he'd miss the events that were important to me, like Christmas and my birthday He'd bring me back presents wherever he went but it was never the same; I guess he was doing his best to make it up to me, but every time he came home I'd have grown-up a little more, wasn't exactly the same kid he'd left behind. And he wasn't the same man either, although his getting older was of an entirely different order to my own. If at first his homecomings were awkward, they could only become more so. And then one day he didn't come home at all. Perhaps a couple of years prior to that I'd stopped asking my mum when he was due back; there didn't really seem any point. He'd turn up when he was good and ready - although she tended to give a few clues in the days before he walked through the door: cleaned the house, bought herself a new dress. That last time he'd been gone about four months before I asked her where he was and when he was coming home. I'd expected her to say Singapore or Freetown or somewhere but it turned out he was in Perth and was staying there - for good. He'd had a heart attack while ashore one day; bang, out of the blue. They'd rung mum and asked her what she wanted them to do with what was left of him and she'd told them he might as well just stay there, no point in him coming back in a state that was of no use to her. Not that was how she replayed it to me, but it was easy enough for me to piece the sequence of events back together. Once she'd told me, I got the impression she was suddenly able to relax, as if she'd been holding onto a grenade she wasn't sure was *not* going to explode. And I suppose it was similar for me; no more strained conversations, unwanted presents - that kind of thing. Until she died, she and I rubbed along pretty well after that. Don't get me wrong, I did miss him in a strange way; his comings and goings had provided a routine of sorts around which we fitted our own lives, though in my case I had the advantage of school providing me with a much more robust framework. None of that mattered to anyone else, of course. I mean, when I went to work for Williams - Benson's predecessor many times removed - the company wasn't interested in your home life, what it had been like growing up, what sort of kid you were; all they seemed to care about was that you had enough O levels and could manage to adequately knot a tie. I guess I scrubbed up well enough. And it was a gentle introduction to the world of work helped by Williams being a bit soft - though I didn't realise that until he had been replaced. Perhaps his aim had been to get through to retirement with as little stress and fuss as possible, so he kept things simple and low-key. As long as the business was trundling along that was good enough for him. But such an approach wasn't acceptable for the new owners who came in some time later; Williams was fired and Johnson-Brown arrived to shake things up. I was in my thirties by then. That was the beginning of a new cycle, and after that every five years or so new owners would steam in with a fresh set of plans, fire the old management team, bring in their own people; we'd rebrand, refocus; there would be a new mission statement, new goals. I was good enough at what I did back then to avoid the fall-out - at least until Benson arrived on the scene. Caroline had been one of Johnson-Brown's recruits. She was tall and as thin as a pencil; not skinny you understand, but she had no hips, and when you looked at her from behind she seemed to be entirely contained within two parallel lines. All of which was exaggerated by what she liked to wear: high heels; narrow, knee-length skirts; tight white blouses. Her breasts were of average size but being the only round things about her, against her general profile they were as prominent as if you'd taken Ben Nevis and dropped it in the middle of the Norfolk fens. Everyone was nice to her, but behind her back they called her Barbie - after the doll - and speculated that she had made herself look the way she did in order to snare a bloke who would be sufficiently blinded to her faults to look after her for the rest of her life - at which point she'd ditch the heels and the skirts and let herself go to pot. They said she was working her way through the department. However brief, I confess I made my pitch too, though I'm not sure where I ended up in the pecking order. Not very high. She finished with me after our second weekend away - to Cromer, it was - her complaints and general demeanour worsening from the Saturday afternoon onwards. I assumed it had been provoked by the squally rain that had blown in off the North Sea. As I recall it now, on the Sunday morning she'd shagged me senseless first thing then told me to go down to breakfast and that she'd see me there. It turned out to be a last hurrah. When she didn't show I went back up to the room to find she'd packed and gone. It was a departure which reminded me of my father. The next day at work it was as if nothing had changed; there she was all straight lines, clip-clopping along the corridors, smiling at most of the men, her hook baited once again. I never told anyone about my dalliance, though I suspect a few guessed given that kind of failure usually left visible scars of some kind. At that time I had no-one to confess to anyway. Mum had died about four years before, leaving me the house to rattle around in. I didn't need three bedrooms, of course, and didn't have the imagination to conceive how I could possibly use them - though if Caroline had worked out, who knows? Had mum still been around she would have seen through her straight away and I'd probably never made it to Cromer in the first place. Anyway, there I was alone in a house too big for me. Briefly I looked into moving to something smaller and more practical, but the mechanics of it appeared just too complicated and unnecessary. Expensive too. All those fees you had to pay, and for what? Yes, I could have sold the house, got something smaller, and had change to spare, but what was the point? Post-Caroline, I actually contemplated telling Johnson-Brown what he could do with his job with one eye on selling up then going off on some adventure - by train and boat, obviously! I told myself I was still young enough - just about - and that it was a perfect opportunity. Who could know where I might end up? And I could always come back, or move somewhere else; buy that smaller house, get a new job in a new place. It might have been good to have been able to walk those ideas through with someone - even George would have done, but he wasn't around then. It might have led to a different outcome. But inertia never really left me. It was too easy to stay in the house, the job; too easy not to think about things, not to take a chance. Oh, don't think I'm a coward. Would a coward have taken Caroline to Cromer, one eye on the 'happy ever after'? I don't think so. Actually, I like to think there was a kind of bravery in staying where I was, that I was achieving something unique; after all, how many people do you know who have lived in the same house for nearly fifty years, man and boy? Mum used to say "a place for everything, and everything in its place". I think she applied that to the both of us, as if the house was providing us our place, and that's where we were supposed to be. If so, then the notion rubbed off on me. The Old Man had no equivalent; the sea was fluid, always moving, and he with it. I think that's one of the reasons mum told the Service he could stay in Australia - he didn't have roots of his own, not really. They certainly weren't in our house, not in any important sense. And when I say I've lived in the house "man and boy", don't think I've kept to the same bedroom for all this time. I started out in the smallest - all the years I don't remember - then graduated to the middle bedroom which was just fine. It had a window that looked out onto the yard, across our small garden with its dilapidated shed, and then down to the back gate and the ginnel beyond. I could see the heads of the dustmen when they came on Tuesdays, ferreting away, dragging those old metal bins by their twisted handles, adding a new dent in each one every week. Once mum had gone I decided I was due a change of scene and allowed myself to graduate to the largest bedroom. In my one gesture of domestic affluence, I paid a three blokes to come in and redecorate the house. Nothing fancy, just a new coat of paint in most rooms, covering up the dated wallpaper. We agreed they would "freshen the place up" and use "neutral, muted colours". They walked me through some colour charts, and having settled on everything pale or off-white, I took myself to Scotland for a week and left them to it. Why Scotland? Well, I'd never been, and you could get there by train. I stayed in Edinburgh most of the time apart from an excursion to Perth where I spent one night. Although I did all the things I was supposed to - the Royal Mile, the castle, Arthur's seat and so forth - I didn't really like it. By the Wednesday I was keen to get back home to see what was happening to the house. Seeing out the week, when I eventually got back I found they had transformed it. Walking through the front door was like one of those corny double-take moments where you think you've walked into the wrong place. It was brighter, modern, clean; it looked like it had escaped from a magazine. The guys had done a super job, really. I'd been sceptical, but they'd known what they were up to. It was then - given that none of the rooms looked like they had previously - that I moved myself into the front bedroom. Thinking about it now, maybe it was actually a bit like moving house - though without actually moving. The only problem was that the new walls made everything else look rubbish; old and dated, out of place. Someone walking in could have been forgiven for thinking that I'd picked up all the furniture on the cheap from a house clearance; that it had all belonged to some eccentric old man who'd just kicked the bucket. It was all so brown! Gradually I began to replace it. I started in the living room, then my bedroom. Money wasn't a problem given the house was all mine - no mortgage - and I had no expensive hobbies on which to waste my disposable income. After about eighteen months I'd redressed the whole place, most of the brown furniture had been banished, and the house looked vaguely modern. Maybe even Caroline would have approved, had she seen it. Mum, on the other hand... Well, it just wouldn't have been her thing at all. I still wonder if she would have regarded it as a betrayal. If the notion of repetitive worlds and permanent purgatory were to be true, perhaps she's somewhere else, presumably in a house looking a lot like this one used to, shaking her head and bemoaning what I've done to the place. They call what I did 'moving on', don't they? And I daresay whoever ends up living here after me will have their own views on decoration and so forth. Maybe they'll be closet Victorians and reinstate floral wallpaper and brown. I'd like to say "I hope not", but the fact is that I won't care. Why should I? One way or another I'll be somewhere else. Maybe I'll have found a new job; one so great that I'll have been happy to up sticks and move, lock stock and barrel - though having said that I find it difficult to conceive of such a scenario. It's not that I can imagine it, of course, it's just that I find it hard to apply it to me; what, for example, would that job look like? What would I be required to do? I know what I can do; it's what I've been doing for years. But lots of traditional admin has been taken away by computers and spotty kids. With that gone - and no desire to return to being a "road warrior"... Well. That was partly Benson's justification for letting me go, the fact that he could get machines to do half of what I did and more quickly and accurately too. It was a point of view I couldn't really argue with. When he coupled that with him recognising I wasn't enjoying the work any more, and, in consequence, was no longer very good at it, then he said the outcome was inevitable. How could I dispute the first of those other reasons given that I hadn't enjoyed working for the firm for some time? But the second part? I still had my moments, occasional triumphs - though they were, I confess, increasingly few and far between. What I needed, I told him, was stimulation; but as it turned out, Benson wasn't in the stimulation game. When George isn't telling me how lucky I am or fantasising about his foreign adventures, he will throw little prompts into our conversations about companies in town who are looking for staff. None of these 'opportunities' are anything like what I'm used to doing, nor would they pay as much, but George assures me they are "not to be sniffed at". The other day - after complimenting me on how I kept myself in shape - he pointed out that there was a warehouse on the business park just outside town who were looking for people. I say warehouse, but I should really say "logistics hub" shouldn't I? For a while I thought George was suggesting some kind of management role until I actually looked into it and discovered he was talking about 'Pick, Pack and Despatch Operatives' - or lackeys with scanners, rather than spanners. However fanciful, that felt a little bit like my life going full circle, me imitating my father - though without the sea, the ships, the travel. Which was enough to rule it out, of course. "So what *are* you looking for?" George had asked when he came back from the Gents, almost as if he had gone there to give himself time to compose his next question. Strange as it may seem, it was an enquiry that struck me as especially valid. Oh, don't think I hadn't asked myself exactly the same thing, but when it comes from someone else, someone 'external', well, it endows the question will a little extra weight. Isn't that right? And therefore, it makes the answer a tad more critical. There are things I don't need, obviously. I have the house - a semi-detached fifties' build in a cul-de-sac that used to look out onto open fields - and my car which, considering the number of miles it has done, I really should think about replacing. I'd managed to buy it cheap from the firm after Benson made it part of my leaving package, getting something else he didn't need off his hands. In addition to motor and mortar, I've no debts to speak of, no responsibilities elsewhere - though that is more by circumstance than design. It might have been nice not to be on my own, to have a wife and kids, to experience the growing up of children from a father's perspective. I do see kids grow up of course, mainly the neighbours', and am always amazed how fast things seem to happen; nappies to school uniforms to falling down drunk on the Market Square in next to no time. Caroline hadn't been my only tentative foray into the foothills of prospective fatherhood, just in case you were wondering. There have been - in Rose, Barbara and Cathy - other brief periods of weak passion and drama. Mum liked Rose, but Rose quickly came to not like us; with Barbara it was the other way round, Mum making sure she spiked that particular drink. After I'd had the house done up I thought I ought to see if I could find someone else who might like what I'd done to the place, someone who'd potentially be happy to live there, fill it with their own things. A divorcee with a six-year-old daughter, I'd met Cathy after responding to her 'lonely hearts' ad in the local paper. Having always wanted to be a nurse but finding herself thwarted by a bastard first husband who abandoned her when Gemma was born, she had made it as far as being a receptionist in a Doctors' surgery. Although not even a half-way house, she liked the work, was good with the patients. I had, I confess, high hopes. But Gemma never took to me for some reason, no matter how hard I tried; and when Cathy found herself having to make a choice between what she might have wanted with me and what her daughter wanted without me - well, there was no contest. She apologised and hoped I'd understand; it wasn't, she said, anything personal. When I told George, he just nodded and offered to buy another round. Based on the outcomes of those various not so near misses, I don't think I'm in the market for another try. Maybe I've become too used to my own company, not having to worry about anyone else; and if that's the case (and remember I have the house, the car) then George's question about what I'm looking for shifts to become "how do I want to fill my time?" - ruling nothing out, of course. Not even adventures by train or boat! Yesterday, for example, I drove the twelve miles or so to our local National Trust property. Considering the scale of their general portfolio it's a rather modest Georgian mansion, but the grounds are nice and the walled garden is splendid. I don't recall us ever going there as a family, and it was only after the Old Man died that mum and I ventured there for the first time. I was too young to be impressed by anything other than the choices offered by the café and the games they occasionally put out on one of the lawns. Mum pretended she knew the rules of croquet and then proceeded to let me win; it had been, I discovered later, a bastardised version of the game. We went once more before she died and then, as part of my reinvention, I decided to become a member of the Trust. It seemed to make sense; I thought doing so would encourage me to get out and about, and initially I had visions of regular weekend trips to places further and further afield. However, the reality is that I was put off by the prospect of driving, so didn't stray far even though I later found myself no longer constrained to going out at weekends. The upshot? I'm something of a regular at the Georgian place these days and try to go once a month to observe the walled garden as it changes across the seasons. They grow some splendid vegetables and have a restored hothouse which, Jack, the Head Gardener, assures me is one of the finest in the Trust's portfolio. He's biased of course, but it's difficult not to be impressed by its wrought iron structure and the clever way the windows in the roof can be opened by turning handles set at shoulder height against the back wall. Although he probably shouldn't have, one day Jack let me have a go at opening them, and having expected them to be really heavy, I was amazed how easily the handle turned and the widows edged open. It was a triumph of ingenuity, I told Jack; he said it was all in the maintenance. For some reason I have tended not to take any photographs in the greenhouse but have started to do so outside. My notion is to compile an album, a kind of log which shows how the walled garden changes across the seasons. It's only for me, of course, and I'm sure Jack and his colleagues have their own record, but they might be interested in what I eventually put together, you never know. On busy days - of which there are few enough - the place is filled with families and picnics, various children and dogs running about uncontrollably. The lawn games are inevitably popular and if you look out from some of the west-facing windows at the top of the house you can see the carnage unfolding below you, the shouts and screams of both children and parents never far away. I was never a particularly shouty child myself. That's not me choosing to remember my childhood in that way but a statement based on the testimony of my mother. When I was well into my teens she told me that she had always been grateful for my placid nature, especially once my father had not come home. It could have been difficult, she confessed, what with her being a single mum and all. There were other mothers she knew - you could pick them out at the school gates, often by their smoking - who always looked tired and harassed; single women struggling under the burden of two or more unruly offspring. For the opposite of a paragon of virtue, she pointed to Jenny Westmacot as the architype of what she herself could have been - and was so glad she wasn't: unmarried, three children by three different fathers, always missing something, like a good coat in winter or proper shoes. But given mum and Jenny were like chalk and cheese there was no way I could conceive of her letting herself go to such an extent that they would become peers. Mum always seemed to have a certain moral standard which she never let drop; it was one of the few things she insisted I try to adopt, and, given I was a pliant child, never something with which she subsequently had an issue. "I'm glad I've only you to worry about," she said more than once, "glad we didn't have more." Personally I've never quite knew how to respond to being told it was a good thing I was an only child. On balance I decided I had the better of things compared to most of my friends at school, especially when I considered the competition some of them faced for attention or presents, or the pain of those bullied by their elder siblings. Yet there was a part of me that occasionally wished I had someone on-hand - a little younger, of course! - with whom I could have gone to the park and play football and such like. Fanciful or not, it was a mild longing that didn't hang around for any great period of time, and as soon as I started studying for my first exams I welcomed the solitude. I was probably fourteen or so when mum started to confess such personal things to me, as if I'd crossed a threshold which allowed her to talk to me in a more mature way and let me in on what she was thinking. Not secrets per se, but that's how they felt at first, and it was a privilege to have them shared with me. I had often wanted to ask her why she hadn't sought to marry again after the Old Man died; I mean, she was still young enough and, although I suppose she was relatively plain, she had a lot going for her - not least the house. I can't remember whether there were ever any suitors, which I guess means there couldn't have been, at least not any that were serious. I always liked Mr. Morris from the corner shop. Friendly, cheerful and generous, he seemed to be the template for the kind of father a boy should hope for. He was also a United fan, and during the summer when there was no football to go and watch, played amateur cricket; once or twice I saw his photo in the local paper, smart in his whites, mid-pose, bat raised as he watched another cover drive laser towards the boundary. Wondering about her marrying again never formed itself into a question, not even later. When did it become too late, either for her to have a new husband or me to be rewarded with a new father? Soon enough, I suspect. There was a narrow window of perhaps four or five years where it might have suited us both, but by the time I'd migrated to A-levels (in which I did rather poorly, by the way) I was already looking over the horizon at what might come next. It wasn't forward thinking or planning as such, but rather the preoccupation of an mildly enquiring mind. There had been conversations about the 'future', a word wrapped in quotation marks and a concept discussed in somewhat hushed tones. From her perspective I suppose the future threatened abandonment - though this time of a more complete nature. If she had loved just two men in her time (and this had been speculation on my part back then), the first one had been deserting her on and off for years until his permanent sojourn in Australia, and suddenly the second was surely concocting plans of a similar nature. Which wasn't entirely true. And as it turned out, I ended up going nowhere at all, taking the easy option of that job with Williams. "Are you sure?" she asked me, trying to disguise how pleased she was that I wouldn't be flying the nest anytime soon. "I'll stay until I really know what I want to do" I told her, convinced that working for Williams would prove to be no more than a holding pattern while I sculpted a far grander plan. Not that such a plan ever materialised - in the same way George's plans for exotic holidays never make it beyond the rim of a pint glass. I suppose I settled quickly, too quickly. Or perhaps I never became unsettled. Work was undemanding; I fell into it easily enough, found myself a niche. Having an income, being able to pay my way, fund the odd treat - a trip out for Sunday lunch perhaps - seduced me into believing that I was in control, biding my time; yet all the while I was being tied down, almost invisibly, like Gulliver when he was on his travels. Except I wasn't going anywhere. And I wasn't in control. I'd given up my freedom for the comfort of a pay-packet and being looked after at home; kidded myself that I would wake up one day and know what I wanted to do with my life and that would be it, I'd be off on adventures. Does it ever happen like that? Before you know it the world has moved on but you haven't gone with it. I mistook change for progress. When Williams went and Johnson-Brown arrived I though the differences he was making were taking us all with him; but they weren't, of course. They were taking him forward, and the business too; a few of my colleagues managed to tag along for the ride. But for the rest of us he represented no more than a slight change in the scenery. What do they say about moving the deckchairs on the 'Titanic'? Johnson-Brown, Caroline, the others that followed them; all markers on my journey, events that one way or another I misunderstood or misconstrued. Whatever 'life' was supposed to be, it was leaving me behind, gradually, surreptitiously. I see that now. Have seen it for a little while. And when you find yourself sitting in a pub with a loser like George speculating over Malta or Madagascar, sipping slightly flat beer - well, it's too late then isn't it? Life's gone flat too. I can hold my end up when it comes to discussing fanciful plans - moving away, a new job, exploring the world - but there comes a point when that's all it is, talk. Because you need something else, don't you? A spark sufficient to make change happen. It takes no spark at all to let others' change affect you. "Try something new," Benson had said as I was about to leave his office. "Look on this as an opportunity for a fresh start." Fresh start? I'm not sure I would know one of those if I tripped over it in Sainsbury's, never mind being able to engineer one on my own. Still, I suppose something might happen one day. I might get a call from a recruitment company who wants to place me in a great business; or I might bump into a nice woman in the shops or at the walled garden, maybe on one of those autumn mornings just as the mist is clearing and it feels as if you can see forever.

The House We Lived In

You want it a little bit tight, he said. Because after a while the skin will lapse.

He means the flesh, the flesh of my fourth finger – how the flesh of my finger will ebb, give way, erode inside this gold embrace. As if the ring will burrow like a tick into my skin, cling, make room for itself, dig in. I find a place to sit near trees, the rain flashes with ice – a fierce clawing into the chalky light, the shreds of pink and green. I think of the child I am carrying. It is a bitter spring.

So they were married, Edith and Luke. They were both very young, Luke the younger by two years. They moved into a shared house on the fringes of a northern city. It was March but no sign of spring. Any daffodils that cautiously opened under the sleety grey skies got their heads whipped back by the wind so that they looked chivvied, unseasonal and sad.

Edith threw up every morning in the bedroom, embarrassed in case she was heard retching, the walls of the house cardboard thin. The other occupants of the house were callow young men – none of whom she knew. Luke was sympathetic and helpful, standing in between her and the rest of the household, and she trusted him with her frailties. But he felt loosened and unanchored missing the small disciplines of the commune where they'd lived previously and where they'd met – falling in love, in desire, precipitously and instinctively.

Before meeting Luke, Edith had been at university, living hand to mouth the way you did then, travelling lightly. In the commune everything was shared; a large warm house, plenty of food; sacks of lentils and brown rice delivered regularly and treats were sweetmeats from the Indian shop on the corner. Things were different now. They were on their own.

Walking through the city streets on a bleak afternoon it seemed to Edith that every other person they passed looked disfigured or crazy. She shied from ugliness, the hard stark lives of this northern city. She felt thin-skinned and exposed, the curled up thing inside her, to which she was not quite reconciled, nevertheless changing her. The two of them were very childish in their relationship and held hands on the top decks of buses and bought pokes of chips.

Luke was obliging, deferring to Edith's condition, her need for beauty, for green; so towards the end of April they hitched south, carrying their belongings in a couple of rucksacks. Anything they couldn't get in got left behind. They didn't have much and only the money given to them as a wedding present by Luke's mother. They gave no thought to the future.

It took all day to reach Devon. Edith was in a macrobiotic phase. She'd made her own wedding cake, so hard and stiff with fruit it was impossible to cut. She thought she might be too yin so had prepared brown rice sandwiches with lettuce to eat on the journey. She felt queasy and querulous – aware that Luke was not dealing well with the uncertainty of their situation.

They lived in a caravan for a bit; sheep rubbing their woolly bottoms up against the sides, rocking it to and fro as they lay in the narrow bed. The Farmer's mother looked askance at Edith's burgeoning shape and thought they were runaways. April into May and the weather turned warm in the southwest, magnolia trees in flower. Edith got the bus one day to the coast; low tide when she arrived and walked straight out into the sea, so magical was the water pooling across the reddish grainy sand of the beach.

They moved into a winter let-down by the seafront in a coastal village. Edith went to child birth classes, took odd jobs; packing at a local factory, counting votes for the referendum. Their life together was fragile, rocky, but the baby arrived early one October morning just as the sun came up. Luke felt faint confronted with the after birth, Edith disorientated and divorced from her body that had somehow delivered, done what it was supposed to do. The child, tiny and perfect, was placed on her stomach as she requested and she held onto its slimy blue and red shape, rather stunned by its physicality, laying claim to possession, already anxious for its welcome, of which she wasn't quite sure.

Surprisingly solid and red, as if you're overdone or peeled, papery scales still sticking to fingers and toes; hair greased to your skull, a gummy whine, mine? These scrawny legs and arms make me think of wish bones. Will they snap? I like it best when folded in a shawl you focus attention like a small saint. Everyone wants to hold you. I'm someone else heady with tiredness, tuned to you — the way you sink into yourself propped up for a burp, head bobbing. The frail stem of your neck.

The baby had been shown the black swans and the lights on Dawlish Water; had matched the cries of the swooping gulls on a winter beach. And they'd made some sort of home there in a makeshift way. The transitory nature of their stay suited Edith. The coastal village was pretty, more so off season. They called the child Tess and Edith walked her into the deeply green park and for a time, looking at the sea every morning, caught in the busyness and wonder of motherhood, found herself content.

Listening, I lie to my baby breathing, bubbling snuffling little chirrups and sighs. She is learning my baby, experimenting with air. Sleeping, your back shaping warm under my hand we are sealed in mute soft dark, folded into this room its night time smells. Stretching, you move slowly, I turn pausing and she floats higher our daughter, safe oh safely. Drowsing, my eyes hush closing — I do not know but she has my heart.

Their tenure in the flat, like Edith's state of mind, was temporary. They had to move on. One of Luke's colleagues told him about a house on the edge of the city and after work one day he went to see it. The house was terraced, street frontage, empty; and cheap. Luke agreed to take it. They arrived one afternoon in January just as it was getting dark, the cold inside astonishing, tomb-like and unrelenting. Edith, carrying the baby well layered-up in a bonnet and jackets, felt stunned by the long grey street lined with cars, the deep chill in the house. This was the future.

Luke had gone to the auction rooms round the corner and bought a table for the kitchen, a double mattress, old and stained, for the bedroom floor upstairs. The sideboard was already in place when they arrived. A solid dark thing that stood in the corner of the kitchen. The initial thought was useful. After all they had no furniture to speak of.

At first Edith stored food inside it, packets of flour, rice, dried beans, tins on one shelf, jars of jam, peanut butter. Then they moved in. Or maybe they were always there and she hadn't noticed them in the obscure dark corners of the cupboard. Long legged spiders excreting a powdery waste, draping each object with nets, shrouds of dust. Slowly Edith, in response, withdrew; stacking the stuff that hadn't been penetrated or defiled on the top, ceding the cupboards to these frail creatures, their pale spores, abandoning the leaked packets too far gone, too doused in scurf, skin, too disappeared. She decided to preserve the presence of this indigenous population; sustain their dry quivering shelter – reflect on perseverance, her own neglect.

Morning in the long cold kitchen, the light from the window bleached and chilly, our only heat this flickering flame blue in the oven's black heart. The child in the sink is as smooth and shiny as a jug, squat next to the scarred pot, its pocked cow's lick of porridge. Above my head nappies steam; the windows are streaming. Down the hall, the shut street door – a car coughs and stutters, belches fumes under the crack. I mash bananas into a field of yellow pleats. Hear the harsh breath of the gas.

Edith didn't know the days, how they began or ended. She knew the struggle of small children, for there were two now. There were delights of course. How could there not be. Mostly these were lyric moments; the fire lit one evening in the small back room and friends gathered for mulled wine and mince pies, racks of greyish wet nappies confined to the entrance passage, the new baby casting her spell of unfolding. Or the days when Edith read Dickens, whilst she breast fed the baby, Dora, and Tess washed dishes at the sink, splashing happily, her bare bottom mottled with cold. She was being potty trained.

Nothing had prepared Edith for her loss of liberty or the relative poverty of their circumstances. She'd fallen in love: and fallen in love also with a way of life that was completely antithetical to that of her parents. Some days she would read 'Seed', an alternative magazine espousing an organic lifestyle and imagined growing herbs in the long narrow stony garden that stretched down to the next street running parallel to theirs. But the garden remained alien territory. The red ants, shiny and barbarous, an alternative life force, colonised the oblong of dandelions, chickweed and wild strawberries. Nettles and thorns scratched and stung if they ventured beyond the backyard.

The relationship was troubled. One day returning to the house from the park Edith looked down the street to see a man with a chair on his head making his way to their front door. It was Luke of course but something in his demeanour, in his effort, made him seem strange, even frightening. He had put money on furniture at the local auction rooms again. The manager once told Edith privately when she had been instructed to call in and discover the result, that Luke's bids were totally unrealistic and he clearly thought Luke more than a little odd in his persistence. However, there was on occasion some yield. They'd acquired a sofa and now an armchair as well as several heavy dining chairs seeded with worm.

Luke had become increasingly morose and unpredictable in his moods. The children left him on a short fuse – impatient and angry. But he wouldn't say why, his face shut in and pasty. He'd always been so beautiful to her Edith thought, his curly hair, slender body and clear skin. They both sought the zeitgeist of the time. 'The Whole Earth Catalogue' had been a wedding gift. Vegetarianism, cooking with love, 'The Tassajara Bread Book'. Living simply. And in peace.

We are stardust
We are golden
And we've got to get ourselves
Back to the garden

So Joni sang in 1969. And maybe that was the only thing they had in common, the 'garden' that Joni sang about. Children of Light.

A like-minded friend moved in for a while, an art student, who populated the outside space, in between the ants and the rampant strawberries, with his ceramics models. Jan was practical and energetic and although he lived on the top floor mostly, he shared the bathroom and took his turn to cook at the weekends, exotic dishes strongly flavoured with herbs and spices. The chaos of the house impinged on him uncomfortably at times. One day he decided enough. Sprinkling the yard with vinegar and water to discourage the ants, he cleaned up the spilt blue fruit juice and the sticky surfaces of the kitchen.

But Edith found she preferred the ants the way they were. She'd liked their disciplined marching file, under the kitchen door, up the wall into that sticky purple pool – the line in place for days, admirable, hypnotic, an endless focused coursing. At least, she thought, they are contained, corralled by the exacting process, distracted from a random criss-crossing of the floor, stinging the baby's plump flesh. She liked their rigour, the ordered pattern of it, a strand to retrieve and come back to.

Edith read a book about bringing up children in the Spanish Alps, where they were fed on goat's milk and white cheese and ran barefoot. Uncertain as always, caught in ambivalence, she didn't know whether to let the girls have the usual vaccinations. Her desire for them to be children of nature, growing up amid grass and trees and flowers, somewhat thwarted by the terraced house, its long hostile garden, the grim car lined street.

Some days we don't get out till dark – by then the park has closed. We stand in the rain watching the trees that seem to be weeping, the long wet hair of their branches sequinned under the street light. Trees, you chant, trees, and we breath in a spicy mulch of leaves, soothed by the soft fall of damp darkness, night deepening over our heads, the walls of the old garden, its tunnel of twisted stems, late roses, withdrawn green lawns. We could be anywhere.

It was not how she thought it would be.

Luke and Edith argued. Her fantasy included a cottage in the country. Luke found such imaginings hard to consider. His family lived in a council flat in the industrial landscape of the steel works – Scotland's central belt. He had no ambition, except perhaps to exist. A dreamer with no dreams. But Luke was right about the vaccinations. They did not, after all, live in the Spanish Alps. Small domestic crises, so woven into the fabric of family life, somehow bound them together. Made something tangible, if not exactly solid, of a tremulous existence, as tremulous as the spiders who lived in the kitchen.

The summer of fleas; weeks of extraordinary weather, the sun merciless on concrete and brick and gutter. The fleas arrived without warning. Shiny backed, curved, they clung to the kids' fat legs as Edith stalked them, pinching between finger and thumb, drowning. Evenings they bounced cockily across the carpet, playing catch me if you can. Edith watched with one eye, ready to pounce, the kids untroubled by the red swellings that rose on their calves, the world too absorbing for sorrow. The cats came and went, scratching their orange fur, shedding fine white dust meant to scour, making them all sneeze. Then suddenly the sun was lower in the sky, losing strength. A few sharp nights and things were back to normal. Luke borrowed next door's vacuum cleaner for extra suction. Edith dressed the kids in socks. And remembered, as if a dream, the days of heat, light, the narrow street alchemized between parallels of cars. The burst of sweetness from cut grass.

Edith couldn't put her finger on when things started to unravel. Maybe it was the day of that curious eccentric sight, the man with a chair on his head at the door of her house. Luke's attitude to spending money and acquiring possessions had become increasingly problematic. Obsessed with making deals, his bids at the local auction rooms continued. As did his erratic and frightening angers. He seemed unable to reflect or account for them. Edith did not perceive Luke's behavior to be aberrational, to have causes that required treatment. Her education, society, had not prepared her for such speculation and she had no way of measuring. She didn't know if it was in her or Luke, this dysphoria, so closely yoked their identities, this joint endeavour of parenthood. Was this married life after all? Was this the way married couples argued, lived their lives? She was left distraught.

The house we live in – chilly even in summer, its long narrow garden jumping with ants. A window box full of butterfly flowers that fell to the street. Days when all the doors of my house hang open, the roof lets in water and there is nothing to be done.

One dark winter's afternoon after a particularly bruising and disturbing scene with Luke, Edith felt a desperate need to talk to someone. Loading Dora into the decrepit buggy held together with masking tape she walked in the cold wet to the nearest phone box. The Samaritans, always there, non-judgmental; but how to begin, how to say it out loud. Was it just a domestic, the way people described such things, would it all be gone the next day? They woke up so many mornings, her and Luke, to find themselves in the same bed, warm, alive, the same small craft of their shared life carrying them forward. And there was no help for it.

You're the folds of my skirt, wrapped round my legs, snot-nosed, sticky fingered, the ground tilting under my feet, mutiny in my heart, and I'm mute. Dumb really – to voice my hollowness into the phone's dark mouth. What can I say caught in the foolish trap of the red box, its stink of piss, the voice on the far end of twisted wire waiting. And I cannot speak. Outside the crazy garish dark of five o'clock, traffic lights flashing, the dazzle of head lamps stinging our eyes. Streets unreeling before us.

Edith marched grimly homewards, thoughts thundering in her head – Tess, like a small animal, trotted after her, her searching face turned upwards. Back to the cold house; the peeling paint and gaps in the skirting boards. The kitchen, the steel framed windows. The small back room with its coal fire. Her life usurped, made sickening. As if she'd built a home on unfounded ground; ground falling away from beneath her. And she couldn't see the fissure it had started from.

At night when the house is still she drops oil into her ears, warming it first, the warm oil slipping into the secret places of her hearing. How lights are low at this time, the world sleeping, her world sleeping. And she savours the room's quiet depths – surfaces in shadow, the doors and windows alcoves of darkness. The warm oil undoes her, so sinuous and golden is its touch.

Grad Student Wife

Michiko steps out of her car into Berkeley cold. The ghostly fog squeezes through her cotton dress and goose bumps rise on her chestnut arms. What a contrast to lunchtime in Palo Alto, her workplace. While running errands in its ninety-degree heat, sweat dampened all her skin. The post office clerk there termed October heat, "Indian Summer" — another new phrase. It's #3 on her list of strange things about California. Despite six years in the Bay Area, and fluency in English, new terms surprise her.

Michiko comes upon her son Masa juggling in a courtyard of Family Student Housing, courtesy of U.C. Berkeley. A boy watching has his buttocks planted directly on the grass — #2 on her list of odd things. Doesn't he realize a dog probably lifted his leg on that green patch?

Her "hello" garners a mere nod from Masa. Michiko misses the grins he tossed her way a year ago. Will he soon cocoon into the surliness of her adolescent daughter? She trudges upstairs. Friday exhaustion earned from three-hour congested commutes — daily. Every step a labor. A cloth grocery bag swings from her shoulder.

Husky voices leak onto their apartment's second-story landing. Her husband Gary and two friends from his Poly-Sci PhD studies have parked themselves at their one and only table. She greets them as she walks in, looking past a partial wall which separates her from the men at their small kitchen table. The guys remain oblivious to her. A #1 on her list of California weirdness. Adults don't greet you. It sometimes feels like she is only a shadow here.

The men blast Bush and his war. Their pungent brew of chips, beer, unwashed bodies, and tobacco overpower the brown rice fragrance, coming from the cooker she set earlier — at 5:30 AM — to finish now. Thirteen hours after her morning departure.

These men she once liked ignored her requests to not smoke too many times. Never saying as much as a thank you after devouring drinks, snacks, and salsa she bought. Why doesn't a guy occasionally bring chips or a six-pack? All they leave are crumbs. Does her husband Gary sweep it up — of course not. They've grated her raw. Anger coils inside Michiko. If Gary paid attention, he'd hear the rattle, but he no longer cares.

No sign of her oldest, Koto, in the living room or her bedroom. She nears Gary. He stops his opining to glance her way. "Hey."

"Where's Koto?"

"I don't know." Gary shrugs. "Probably at Sky's."

These days both Gary and her daughter dwarf Michiko. Koto at five feet eight towers over her, and the tight tees Koto selects outline her breasts. An innocent disguised in an adult body. Though Michiko is glad Koto has a good friend, she'd prefer her daughter keep out of Sky's home. Once the girl came to their home with runny mascara shadowing her pale cheeks. Michiko brought snacks and listened to the girl. Sky admitted tearfully that she'd discovered her grad-student mom naked in the arms of a man, not her husband. Michiko found it abhorrent. Sky's dad worked and paid rent so the mother could study — a lapse of loyalty and gratitude.

Michiko gives Gary a hard stare, as if to say, *you should be keeping track of Koto*, then jerks open the refrigerator door. In goes the half gallon of milk and out stays the tofu. Michiko's gnawing questions don't disturb Gary. Will their daughter do her homework? What values shape her?

Normally Michiko would take on the job of arranging details of her children's lives, but she can't. Gary takes his UC Berkeley grad classes, while Michiko works full-time to pay the bills. Gary doesn't do much while she's away. He disappears from the kids and meanders through his studies. Eight years he's been at it. The feedback from the professors isn't good. Even if he does eventually get their approval, will he ever find a job in the Poly-Sci field? Michiko has concluded he lacks the discipline to finish his dissertation. Or is it lack of courage?

Her cell rings. The boss speaks in Japanese, his preferred language.

"My schedule changed. Cancel the flight. Book it for Tuesday. ASAP."

No apologies for calling at 6:15 on Friday. Not even the polite Japanese term for, *please do me a favor*?

"Call me when you get them."

They sign off. Gary glances her way and sees her opening her laptop.

"Well, guys, I guess I better get to work. The wife is still at it." The men head out with a few claps on the back and see you next week.

"Gary, you know I don't like Koto over at Sky's. Go get her, please."

Koto walks in later with Gary, Masa close behind. Koto thrusts out lower lips in silent anger. Still, when Michiko asks — ever-so-sweetly — Koto washes and chops vegetables, freeing Michiko to purchase the boss's plane ticket. Gary assists his daughter, but when Michiko starts the stir-frying, he goes to watch TV.

The four sit at the table. The scent of charred beef and onion, the richness of carrots, greens, saké and soy sauce have driven out the unwanted odors.

"I got a part in 'Mousetrap' as Mollie." Koto lifts her freckled cheeks to her dad.

"Super." Gary gives her a high five.

But Michiko merely jostles a knee against the table's rough underside.

"Mother, aren't you going to say, 'Congratulations?'"

"The play will get in the way of bringing your grades up, won't it? You need good grades to earn a scholarship for college. We won't have enough." Michiko eyes Gary, then Koto. "What did you get on the last math quiz?"

"C+." She glares. "There was stuff he didn't tell us to study."

"I'm paying for math Kumon and you only get a C!" Michiko clunks her barley tea down.

Koto draws herself up. Even seated, she's taller than her mom. She aims her gaze at Michiko's breastbone.

Gary lifts a glob of rice to his mouth. "What is it — a whole two weeks since she's started meeting her math tutor?"

"Three weeks."

"So? Give her time."

The exchange of smiles between Gary and Koto stings. Tea to a canker sore. Gary's sympathy has melded with Koto's wilfulness. A combined force. And her efforts to move Gary to think long-term have always sunk into the ocean of his oblivion. His *enjoy the moment* mentality blocks Michiko from nudging Koto toward the needful.

Michiko must gaman again, rather than provoke Koto's contempt.

A toothache has bothered her in recent weeks — off and on. Her dentist says, *Wait till it's steady.* Again it pokes. Michiko groans.

"Why does my tooth ache now? Kras works only weekdays." Her dentist from Poland.

"Take some Tylenol," Gary says.

Michiko finds and swallows a red tablet from the bathroom medicine cabinet. Sitting, she watches her family eat slices of carrots and bok choy, but takes nothing. It would hurt too much. "Masa, how is school going?"

Her boy shrugs. Masa doesn't do assignments without prodding, and she worries he'll turn out like Gary and like Gary's dad. He too has never worked since marriage. Isn't determination to support yourself a good thing?

Honks of cars blast through the thin walls. The odor of pot seeps through their poorly-caulked windows. Oh, for more than student housing.

A text dings. Koto retrieves her cell. Her blackish brown hair falls to graze her lap. Michiko hears Sky's voice coming through the phone.

"Yes. Yes." Koto looks only Gary. "Sky is asking me to a movie."

"What movie is it?" asks Michiko.

"Tangled."

"PG?"

Koto sighs. "Of course. It's Disney! I just need a ride. Sky's already downtown with Linda."

Linda is Sky's mom, the name she told Koto to use. Oddity #4, the way adults allow kids to treat them. Michiko nods approval to the outing.

"Gary, can you stay here with Masa? I'll drop off Koto and meet a friend."

"What do you say, Masa? We can watch a guy's show." Gary taps Masa on his bicep.

Paused at a stoplight, Michiko turns to Koto. Purple colors her eyelids. When Michiko was thirteen, she didn't wear eyeshadow. Schools forbade it. For a school to allow eye makeup and nail polish was oddity #5. "You'll only go to the movie, right?"

"I don't know. Maybe we'll go out for fro-yo."

"That boyfriend of Linda's — will he be there?"

"I don't know." Koto stares out the window. "Mother." She stretches out the two syllables, sliding from high to low. "It's not like you and Dad are perfect. Besides, this is Berkeley, not rural Japan."

Koto speaks of Michiko's hometown. The countryside she escaped for a high-ranking high school. And that enabled her to qualify for a top Tokyo public university. There she met Gary, a conversation partner for an English major like her, and she helped him with his studies in Japanese.

"Right is still right." Michiko can't tolerate what Koto implies. The way she and Gary argue or ignore each other don't compare to betrayal. Michiko has always been faithful

"You're mean as Grandma!"

The dig stuns. Michiko's head shakes, trying to slough it off. She glances at Koto who holds a hairbrush. Leaning forward, her daughter casts her thick, long strands over her head like a mask. Except for the rake of Koto's brush, the car trembles with silence. Michiko wonders, are her distinctions mean?

Is she like her mother?

A car honks. The light has changed. Michiko mashes down on the accelerator. The car jerks.

"My gawd," Koto peers at her through an ashen curtain.

Michiko's chest tightens. Breathing is arduous. The blocks she drives constrict. Cars, fumes, and angst mingle on the way to the theater. In time she nears it, pulls over, and hands Koto eight dollars.

"That's only enough for the movie, Mom."

Michiko digs to find another five — the word "Mom" means "give." Michiko's remaining cash will cover only one drink. It ends the last of their weekly budget. Michiko will gaman. A credit card is not for entertainment.

"Thanks." Koto's slam of the door belies gratitude.

A few more lights while wetness clouds Michiko's vision of the street signs. A consummate fault-finder, her mother seldom praised. She's why Michiko crossed the seas.

Michiko's whole jaw aches. The infected tooth ratchets up its pain. She calls to mind the mandarin tree of her countryside home, her escape then and now. Once again, the sense of sitting within its leafy bower and smelling sweet citrus brings relief. Immersed in green, she almost misses the neon sign spelling "Beckett's" above the bar's rough timber doors.

Michiko discovers a parking spot, and then Ji Eun outside of Beckett's. They squeeze through the mélange of blondes, brunettes, redheads, turning sideways at times. Twangs follow a strange wail floating out from the band.

They perch at a tiny table. Michiko feels the warmth of Ji Eun's examination of the set of her brow, her lips. "I think you need a drink."

This bright woman knows her. Like Michiko, Ji Eun is married to a grad student, but his Korean company supports his studies at UC Berkeley. A native of Korea, Ji Eun once taught college psychology classes there. Here she assists at her toddler's preschool.

"Yeah. I've got a toothache."

"Oh, terrible. What have you taken?"

"Tylenol. I'll try ibuprofen next." She reaches for the bottle in her purse.

A waitress in a fitted waist dress sets down drink menus.

"I need water." The waitress nods.

Michiko peruses the drink menu and doesn't notice when their glasses of water land on the table.

"Ladies, what can I get you?"

"A Regina Spektor please." Michiko points to the name in case her pronunciation is wrong.

"Any food?"

"No, I'm fine." Ji Eun cocks her head at Michiko, and then orders Shamrock wings and blue cheese fries in addition to a Lonnie Jordan. It's double her normal and cheesy fries are Michiko's favorite. She figures Ji Eun guesses her money situation.

Ji Eun excuses herself to the ladies' room. Michiko admires her stiletto walk and slim hips highlighted in tight jeans. She's as chic as the Todai college students were back when Michiko, in hiking boots, clunked up the steps of academic buildings. The outlet or Uniqlo attire, all she could afford, attracted few friends. Any Koreans were off her radar, but here in Berkeley Michiko feels a commonness with Ji Eun, both mothers and foreigners within the FSA complex.

The waitress taps down two glasses: Ji Eun's blood orange and Michiko's somber red. Its bubbles spread, rise, and pop. Ji Eun seats herself, and Michiko lifts her glass. "Let's toast." After they click glasses, Michiko keeps her glass suspended. It creates an exaggeratedly rounded image of Ji Eun. Michiko has watched a few of the Korean soap operas that are the rage for Japanese women. They swoon for the male Korean stars.

If Michiko had married Korean, would her life seem afloat? A Korean father would expect his children to study hard.

The myriad of mandates of her homeland have long exasperated Michiko, any relaxation of etiquette bringing criticism. Those fashion dictates of Tokyo girls that caused Michiko's exclusion. Sandals labelled dangerous.

Dating Gary meant strictures removed. Disapproval vanished.

"Take some." Ji Eun nudges her fries towards Michiko. "How is work, Mi-chan?"

Michiko melts at that name of endearment. With Ji Eun, she uncloaks what she stopped showing Gary. "Bad. Kojiro-san got real mad when I was late. It was an accident — I couldn't help it!"

"Ahh, keu-lu-koon-yo," — Korean empathy. "Your long commute."

Michiko savors a bumpy cheese fry. "No job here for me. No American boss wants imperfect English. And Japanese is for Stanford and Palo Alto, not Berkeley. No startups here, only in Silicon Valley." Michiko draws out the location, while pulling her eyes wide as a dazzled tourist. She pretends to take a photo. Ji Eun giggles. "No way to work here." Michiko makes a fish pout.

Ji Eun sighs. "It's all you can do. When Gary finishes, life will be easier."

"If he does." Michiko has hidden Gary's laziness and the lies. "How's your daughter?"

Ji Eun shrugs. "She likes preschool and I like helping. The kids are cute, but I miss lecturing and conversations about ideas." Ji Eun lowers her thick lashes. "And your kids?"

"Koto pisses me off. Today she said I was like Okah-san." Michiko bites her lip, surprised at what she's admitted.

Ji Eun's silence scares Michiko. Her friend is studying the "Shamrock" wing she dis-assembles, rather than reassuring her it's not true. Michiko purses her lips around her straw. The wail of the music crescendos.

Ji Eun leans in to speak, a whisper as demanding as a kettle's whistle. "What do you think she meant?"

Oh, that Michiko could ease her twitching thighs by hustling away. But Ji Eun has long been her best friend. A violin moans and Michiko loses herself in it for a moment, yet Ji Eun's eyes compel Michiko to respond.

"That I grumble a lot. About her, about Gary." She leaves out how she instructs her husband in how to keep the household running, and how that bugs Koto. Michiko lifts her glass and gulps.

"It's easy to repeat our childhood experiences."

"Gary is repeating what his father did! Never a job! His wife did all the work. Gary talks bullshit with friends while I slave. Friday nights he watches one movie after another. I fall asleep on the couch. Always exhausted." She doesn't mention the foot of space between them.

Ji Eun's eyes, grown wide as orbs of a chestnut, offer the sympathy Michiko needs.

"Sometimes I think about divorce." She bottoms up her glass. It's the first time she's used the word. Offspring nail two adults together, building a home. Marriage is not about amorous feelings.

Michiko's friend keeps her face very still, yet her leg shifts. A giveaway as to her tension.

"Without Gary, no campus housing. Rent triples. And I can't sacrifice my kids' education. Or give up lessons or college."

"You stay for Koto and Masa."

Michiko nods. She thinks of their trips to Japan and backpacking vacations. Their outings have bought smiles and memories, a joy she didn't know as a child. On a single income, no such.

"Perhaps happiness is possible for you and Gary. A marriage counselor is not so expensive on campus."

"You think it's my fault." Michiko caps the spring welling inside.

"No, no. Like we Koreans say, 'Both palms make a clap.'"

"I can't." The image of talking about private issues with someone she doesn't know makes Michiko feel like throwing up.

"It's difficult for Koreans. Our shame. Perhaps Japanese feel the same?"

Michiko doesn't know a single person who's seen a counselor or would admit it.

The rippling notes of the accordion stop. The violin again laments.

"Talking about pain and conflict is tough, but brings new ways. Maybe relief." Ji Eun cranes so that her face only centimeters away. "A counselor could help Gary understand your point of view, and" — Ji Eun pauses to stare at Michiko; eventually Michiko nods slightly, permission for her friend to go on — "help you understand your own reactions. You'll see what's hidden inside, like an x-ray."

These words poke Michiko worse than Kras with his shiny dental probe. She hates feeling powerless. She's too short to jump down from a dental chair levered up high. It traps her. And she abhors the plastic rectangles a hygienist shove inside her soft mouth. They cut and torment her while they x-ray.

Kras's question in her last dental check-up pops up. *When do you think Gary will finish? It's been four years, hasn't it?* Direct and pushy questions — oddity #6. The dentist's words kept her rolling from side to side in her bed at night. Gary slept, heedless of the future. He's always shoved away her questions as to how they will pay for their kids' education.

A single red teardrop rolls down the curve of her glass.

"I'm sorry. I'm a bother," says Michiko.

"No, you help me too." Ji Eun's earrings swing as she denies Michiko's need to apologize, shaking her head. "Doesn't your long commute make you tired?" Michiko nods. "Could you get a room in Palo Alto for the weekdays?"

"But the cost!"

"You'd save on gas, and time. Maybe a friend might loan you a room?"

Michiko flashes on a single woman — generous, with a two-bedroom Palo Alto house.

"Would Gary protest?"

Michiko rolls her eyes. "Shouldn't make a difference. Washing his shirts and putting dinner on — that's how far marriage goes."

The violin's wail evaporates.

＊

She wakes to a silent bed. The middle is hers. Coldly and frighteningly hers. She'd been dreaming of her middle school graduation, wearing a burgundy dress. So proud then to know she qualified to leave Seiwa for a special high school. Youthful dreams of glory have bled away.

After three nights here she's used to the brisk steps of Teresa who owns this home. To how Teresa dresses for a daily six-a.m. jog. Michiko's drive to work has become trivial — ten minutes. She gets eight hours of sleep, and still has time to call Masa and Koto. But her tooth still aches despite constant rounds of ibuprofen. It somersaults her stomach. She can't gaman this one.

A new dentist, the one Teresa sees, will see her at 4:00 p.m. in Palo Alto. She's asked Gary to take Masa to fencing and Koto to her Kumon session.

Michiko walks into the student housing courtyard at 7:00 p.m. after a dental appointment. Masa's ball drops in the hoop, and then he explains that Gary wasn't around to take him to fencing. Upstairs, Koto studies lines for the play. Gary didn't come home, so no math practice at Kumon. Michiko dials her husband, but no answer.

Books and jackets are strewn across the couch and living room floor, on the kitchen counter dishes stacked to teetering heights. She glares at the iron skillet with blackened bits sitting atop a spaghetti pot on the stove. She'll ignore the cleanup for now and get dinner on. The dishes will grow to mountain size. After dinner she'll tackle them — no Friday night relaxing. When she sits down for dinner hours, her jaw hurts. The dentist had suggested ibuprofen before the pain killer wore off, but she forgot. She's ready to sink her teeth into any threat to her cubs. After dinner and dishes, she wheels the rust-pocked Hoover, sucking up bits of chips. A thick hand of resentment pushes against her chest.

Gary appears half-way through her sweep.

"Where have you been? You didn't get the kids to their lessons! Or even call about dinner."

"I had to bunker at the library to study — what with being Mr. Mom 24-7."

"But Koto missed Kumon, and Masa kendo. We've paid for them!"

"Give me a break. If you care so much, why weren't you here?" Gary grabs a container from refrigerator and makes to leave.

"I got my cavity filled!" Her voice crescendos.

Koto goes to slam her bedroom door.

Gary leaves. In bed later, Michiko slumbers alone. When fingers of light touch their room, the rasp of his breath and his yeasty alcohol scent penetrate her consciousness. She sees his blond strands spread on the pillowcase, and the pale of his forearm thrown her way. A thread of blue runs its length, a fragile line of life. There was a time when he drove her to the hospital, while her thumb hung half off. "I'm sorry," she said repeated for the crimson on the car, his shirt.

It doesn't matter. Only you matter, his words. She knew then he loved her. Gratitude laced their bodies together.

But last night, her bitter voice repeats itself inside her head. She had good reason — but wasn't that how Okah-san justified the jagged points thrust her way? Didn't resentment war within her? Perhaps Michiko has become like her. Ji Eun's words reverberate like a whirring drill. *It takes two hands to clap.*

Michiko wipes a rough tissue under her eyes. Gary sleeps on. While she brews coffee, makes eggs, and eats with the children, he slumbers. Masa goes outside with basketball under arm, while Koto stays to stare at her script and mutter softly. Michiko is collecting dirty laundry when Koto approaches.

"It's sunny. Let's all do something." Koto coils a strand of hair around her finger.

A groan is burning its way up within Michiko when Okah-san flashes in her mind — leaning over the sink or hunched over gardening. "Hatarakimono" — always working she'd called her. As a teen bitterness mushroomed for the fun she'd missed.

Michiko releases her dishwashing sponge and her eyes lock on to the chocolate brown ones of Koto. A girl influenced by Berkeley friends. "Want to picnic?"

"Yeah! Like we used to."

"Can you make the rice balls?" Michiko had started rice thirty minutes ago and its warm, thick fragrance fills the air. They've learned to work side by side on the small countertop. Michiko coats and fries chicken, its hefty aroma of grease and spice overpowers other smells.

Gary's footsteps thud in the hallways. He sniffs near the two.

"Hey, Dad."

"Good morning," Michiko forces out.

"Yeah, morning." Wearing his old sweatshirt and cut-offs, he stares at the lunch box with its compartments. Cherry tomatoes tucked against chicken morsels. Triangles of rice wrapped in green-black seaweed, glistening with salt.

"Wow. Fried chicken. Let's picnic."

On their way to Tilden Park, they don't converse. When Gary follows a truck closely, Michiko says nothing, but her foot presses hard on the rubber mat. Taps come from Koto's fingers flying over her keypad. Blips from Masa's Game Boy.

Cars occupy the parking slots at their favorite picnic area. Gary curses. He searches elsewhere for parking, after the rest get out. At least their familiar picnic table stands vacant. Sunlight lights up initials Gary once carved on its well-grained surface. Masa starts for the lawn with the Frisbee. When Gary reappears, the blue saucer glides back and forth seamlessly.

"Let's go to the carousel," Koto urges Michiko.

Koto once adored it and Michiko can't refuse. She calls out to Gary and Masa, now wrestling on the grass, and they enter the warm dark of the grove. Fallen needles underfoot give way and release a pine smell combining with the woodsy fragrance of the redwoods.

"I've got a new classmate, Danish."

"Great. What's her name?"

"Ada."

"Be nice to her. She's an outsider, like we are."

Michiko pauses in search of where a woodpecker's rap issues. Past a downed tree, she spots a small bulb-like tree of rich green, standing out against the grayish hue of pines. Why has she not glimpsed that tree before, so like ones of her home orchard? Michiko wants a closer look, but it's not on route to the jangling music of the carousel, a faint but persistent call.

"I'll have Ada over next week."

They leave the dark coolness of the grove, walking within a small meadow of copper-brown grass.

"The house will be a mess! It's a terrible first impression."

Koto shrugs. "And I'll pick up my stuff." Michiko snorts. "And make Masa pick up his."

Michiko harrumphs. "How about Gary? And the dishes"

"I was so busy last week. Dad told me to help Masa with his math and he didn't listen. It sucks."

Michiko holds back her critical words. A painful pulse comes from the newly-filled cavity.

They stop at the meadow's edge. The carousel circles six yards away. Old and young sit on the horses, lions, and zebras; others stand aiming cameras. Bystanders ring it, some snapping photos.

"He had to correct papers." Koto's foot digs at the dirt. "You know, the class he T.A.'s."

"He should do that earlier during the day and help you at night."

"His library job and lectures. He made dinners anyway." Koto tosses her hair, like a horse chafing under its reins. "I did the dishes by myself sometimes."

"When I was in high school, I picked mikan after school for hours! I drank tea and pinched myself to stay awake as I studied at night."

"Mom." A two-syllable descent. "That was Japan. This is America. Besides, your mother wasn't staying in another city."

Michiko clenches her teeth. She swallows her anger at Koto, and thinks, *no appreciation for how hard I've always worked.*

The carousel groans to a stop. A parent steps off her zebra and helps a small boy with tow-colored curls clamber off his elephant.

"Do you want to ride?" Michiko hopes it will break their dance.

Koto is silent, her face like granite. Her eyes follow her old-time favorite carousel figure, a zebra, now without a rider.

Michiko wonders what it means to not be like Okah-san. At least she hasn't repeated her mother's words: I work day and night so you can have better opportunities than me. Michiko's thighs quiver, but she roots herself.

"For old times' sake will you join me?"

Koto steps up to the zebra. Michiko pays.

The unicorn standing near her daughter's mount invites her. She fingers its gold horn, and recalls earlier dreams. The stuff of fantasy — golden California.

"Dad works harder than you think."

Her daughter needs to see Gary this way, Michiko thinks, her lips frozen hard. She stares off at the anomalous tree she'd noticed.

Jaunty music begins. The unicorn's slow circling brings comfort. The prickling of her thighs eases. The growl of gears stops.

"Once more?" she asks Koto and she shakes her head.

Once again on the ground, Michiko feels lighter. Koto seems breezier too. The two stroll back.

"I hate having you and Dad fight so much."

"When I'm away, we don't fight." They're in the comfort of trees now.

"Some solution." Koto's eyes turn like a carousel. "Can't you stop being so hard on us!"

"I can't keep up the commute. I'm exhausted."

"Screw you." Koto's jean-clad legs speed up, kicking up and away, aimed at Gary.

Michiko holds back a yell. It's the first time Koto has cursed her and dampness fills her eyes. Demanding an apology would bring nothing good.

She walks away from the path and toward the incongruous tree. A close up view confirms her far away impression. Its dark, broad leaves shine. She whiffs a familiar fragrance, and fingers a glossy leaf, almost round. A hard, emerald ball hangs from a stem. A Hachiya persimmon. In a few weeks the un-giving balls will turn light orange. In a month or more, a deep orange. She'll return to pick some and let them soften at home. Eventually she can spoon out sugary-sweet pulp, a pleasure of home. An ache arises within.

Perhaps if the rancor at home continues, she'll return to her rural home and its orchard. She'll take care of it and her parents when they're frail. The fruit trees will be hers again. Will she still be agile enough to climb a mikan tree? To sit within its green fans of leaves while orange globes dance before her.

A child's wail comes. Her seven-year-old face streaked with tears comes unbidden — Michiko peering in the mirror after Mother's cruel words and, to hide the tear streaks, splashing water on her face. And Kras's question still pesters. The how and why of her coming to America.

Of course Gary's tall and muscular body, the stroke of his hand pulled her in. She remembers how proud she felt to have an American lover, and how sweet it was that he loved her hiking boots paired with short dresses, her counter cultural fashion. But how much of it was rebellion against Okah-san?

She returns to the picnic table. It lies shaded. A bulk of gray obscures the sun. Her family is eating. They didn't come to call her. How rude, how unwanted she feels.

"The chicken's yummy, Mom. Masa was eating it up quick, but I saved you some." Koto gets up from her place next to Gary and goes to Masa's side.

Michiko seats herself on the splintery surface, though she feels her thigh quivering at being so close to Gary.

"Thanks for the yummy lunch." says Gary. "Like old times." Michiko meets his smile and nods. "I met with Professor Ronaldson this week. He likes what he's seen so far of my thesis."

Koto glows. She believes her dad.

Michiko doubts that Gary tells the truth. She's caught his lies before. She's seen him hanging out with friends instead of studying. She knows what he wants — her to be happy with him. He wants her in bed, close to him tonight.

She shivers in the cooling air, the clouds over the sun. Gary puts his arm around her, touching then not touching, his uncertainty palpable. She gives in. Her head against his shoulder brings some warmth. His chin against her head, bristles pricking. This a moment's truce — she needs him to change.

Michiko savors the rice ball she bites, its sesame and nori flavoring. "Great rice balls!" She grins at Koto.

"Thank you." The tight, creased places around Koto's eyes soften.

After lunch Michiko spreads a picnic sheet, a pink and white plastic purchased at Tokyo's Daimaru Department store. Head down, face up, she stares at the tips of redwoods and oaks. Thuds and exclamations travel from the field where Gary, Koto and Masa play ball. Exhaustion no longer pounds her body. Her cavity was bored and filled, despite how her thighs twitched on that dental chair.

Michiko shifts her head and sees Masa batting a ball. Fleet-footed Koto runs and grabs high in the air for it. Her dad cheers both of his kids. They are obviously loving having the picnic and parental peace.

Perhaps she will ask Gary to join her, while she suspends herself, trembling on a counselor's chair.

The Vines

The Vines

Residents. A baffling species. They act in unexpected ways. One moment they fill your walls with light, laughter, love, then they vanish, leaving others to clear up their mess.

Since the day of the Terrible Event my inhabitants have been few and far between, however. Occasionally there were squatters, students, sightseers. But largely the human species have kept away. Until today. The wind moans just like it did that day. Rain beats against my roof, people rush past, gabbling into their phones and gadgets. Then I spy her. A previous inhabitant. Plumper, older, sadder. She reaches the overgrown hedge surrounding these walls, attempts to peer over the top, but it's too high. She shrugs, then wanders on, frowning at the smartphone in her hand.

Starlings gather around my chimneys, cats leap up and down the patchwork walls, lights go on in other houses. Rain lashes harder, dripping down gutters, leaking through my roof.

The ex-inhabitant puts up her hood, dashes across the road. A car hoots, the driver shouts an obscenity. She reaches the end of the street and disappears round the corner.

Poppy

The corner café. Cliff and I would stop by on our way home from school, squander pocket money on sausage rolls, stringy cheeseburgers and cigarettes. Now it's a vegan café; warm, bright, empty. The guy behind the counter is packing away cakes and wiping tables. I order a double espresso and a muffin and say my brother will be joining me. I tell him we used to come here before it changed hands. The days when tea was either weak or strong and coffee was black or white.

"I only took this place over last year," he says. "On sunny days you have to queue for table."

"I'll bear that in mind," I say. Although I've no intention of returning.

Wolf

So this is what happens. I get chucked off the bus cos I only have cash. The driver eyeballs me coins as though they're antiques.

"Oyster card?" he barks.

So I tell him I can't afford oysters but could kill for a rare steak. He yells at me to get off his bus or he'll radio for assistance. Wanna give him what for but I'll only end up back in trouble. So I jump off, find myself in some fancy area. Chelsea. All twee shops, posh houses and the like. Tempting, so tempting. Then I spy an off-licence, nip inside to pick up some cans of bitter. But they don't want me dough neither.

"Cards only," says the poxy cashier.

So I tell the git no-one sends me cards no more. Not even me old Mum. He ignores me, serves the next customer. I threaten to give him what he deserves. Just a threat, you understand but he creates merry hell so I get out of there quick, before he spots me rucksack bulging with bottles of vodka. No-where to hide, rain pissing it down, so I duck into this caff. Some bird sits staring out of the window. So I join her.

Cliff

Hi Pops, sorry I'm so late. stuck on train between Hyde Park corner and Knightsbridge. Be there soon as I can. Promise.

She won't believe me. Never does. Why do I bother? The message won't even send. No signal. And now my laptop's out of battery, I can't even catch up on work. Utter waste of my valuable time. A sign that I shouldn't be making this journey.

Poppy

The coffee makes my heart race. I sip it slowly, savouring the sugar-rush from the muffin. Cliff should be here by now. Why won't he reply to my messages? The guy behind the counter keeps glancing at me, checking the time, wiping the espresso machine, polishing the same glasses. I order a second espresso. And a third. They probably need the business. Another customer comes in, soaked, bedraggled. He gazes at the specials board, glances around, then approaches my table. He smells unwashed.

"I'm waiting for someone," I tell him.

"Do us a favour, eh, love? Thing is, me wallet's vanished. I've had nothing to drink all day and I'm famished."

I see the owner watching. It goes through my mind that he must think this tramp is my brother. I decide to play along. It could buy me time.

Cliff

Knightsbridge Station, finally. Traffic gridlocked, not a vacant cab in sight. I contemplate walking but then the heavens open. This is crazy. Still, she needs to get it out of her system. She's the one who gets the nightmares, not me. I was able to shut it out. Eventually. Got on with life.

Poppy

I buy him a tea; he wants plain builders' variety. He constantly adds sugar as he sips and talks. He's been living on the streets, he says.

His parents perished in a car crash when he was three. No other living relatives. For some reason I find myself talking about it. The Vines. He knows its history. Doesn't everyone? He assumes I'm a prospective buyer. I'm completely unaware of the tears running down my face until he asks if I have a connection to the house, an emotional one. So I tell him the truth. He's very understanding, he knows what it's like to lose both parents suddenly. I explain that although I was thirteen at the time, I have little memory of my life before it happened, in fact I can barely picture Mum and Dad's faces. I'm hoping standing inside the house I grew up in will awaken memories of better times. He asks if I'd like him to accompany me but I tell him my brother is meeting me at the house. If I find it. But then a house can't just vanish, can it? He starts to laugh and for some reason I find myself laughing too.

Wolf

The Vines, eh. Well, well. The notorious Vines. Know all about that place. Me good mate Jonno, wrongly convicted. A lifer. All the mates knew he was innocent. The general consensus was that it was someone from inside the family. No way was that a professional job. So, she's the daughter. Well, well.

The café geezer says he has to close up, chucks us out. I wish her luck and we go on our separate ways. Least, she does. I stand in the doorway looking at the list of hostels they give us, trying to work out how to call them on this mobile I've forgotten how to use. Then, ping… an idea hits us. A bolt from the blue.

Cliff

I'm on a bus when Carol calls. An emergency, well isn't it always? Katie was sent home from school with a temperature, she has a management meeting in half-an-hour. I remind her I'm doing this for Poppy. Never mind your hysterical sister, she says. Doesn't your daughter come first? If you don't message her, I will.

Poppy and Cliff

"Are you too much of a coward to call?"

"I'm on a packed bus."

"I should have guessed you'd chicken out."

"Katie's sick. What am I supposed to do?"

"Find a better excuse."

"I'm still not convinced this is a good idea, Pops."

"Ah, so that's it."

"You could have a relapse."

"That's why I want you to come with me."

"Ask the agent to accompany you. Remember, as far as they're concerned we're prospective buyers."

"But we're not. Supposing I break down?"

"Look, if you can wait around, I'll see if Katie's ok with being left."

"I spent twenty quid on an off-peak return. If I miss the seven-thirty back I'll have to pay double. You'd better turn up, Cliff, because if you don't ... Cliff? Don't hang up on me!"

The Vines

The rain is subsiding. Shoppers leave doorways and shelters, rush-hour queues form at bus-stops; cars slosh their way through rainbow puddles, splashing passers-by.

My ex-inhabitant makes her way back down the street. So, she's worked it out. The flats are newly built. The building site next door used to be numbers seventy to ninety-two. Few of the houses have names these days. Most are divided into flats, their inhabitants are younger, scruffier. Always rushing here and there.

She stands on tip-toe, peering into these dark windows then she hunts for the gate, which has been swallowed up by the hedge. She walks towards my front entrance as though in a trance, completely unaware of the fellow coming up the path behind her, swigging from a beer can.

Poppy

As I climb the steps to the front door I find myself listening for 'Fido' to start barking. We didn't really have a dog, it was just a recording, set off by a wire beneath the mat. I rummage through my pockets for the key. Not there. Then I realise I'm looking for the fluffy bunny keyring that my thirteen-year-old-self owned, ignoring the key with the Sloane Square Estates label tied to it.

The teeth of the key dig into my hand as I try to force it into the lock.

"Need a hand?"

I smell beery breath, turn to see the weird guy from the café standing behind me.

"No, I'm fine. Thank you."

"So this is it, eh. The Vines."

"Actually, if you have a strong wrist, could you try to turn this key"

"No problem."

He spits on the key and gives it a yank but the lock won't oblige.

"You've been given the wrong one love."

"Are you sure? Typical. I'll give the agent a call."

He stands watching as I listen to the ring-tone and then the message cutting in saying they're closed.

"It doesn't matter," I tell him. "I'll leave it."

"I'll get you in there in no time."

"How?"

"Easy, show you."

He takes a pen from inside his pocket, it has some gadget attached. He has the lock unscrewed instantly.

"There you go love." I'll re-attach it while you're inside, then I'll be on me way."

"That's great, thanks for your help."

"Pleasure."

Cliff

Hi Pops. Katy is lying down with a temperature. I'd better not leave her. You can do this on your own. Call me once you get inside.

Poppy

The hallway is littered with leaflets and unopened letters. I push open the door to the living room. It's coming back to me. The flies, the smell, the mess. Fragments of Mum's sculptures scattered over the carpet. Dad's drinks cabinet fallen; rivers of whisky streaming from shattered bottles. I can hear the high-pitched hum from the phone, its receiver dangling. Then the scene fades into the floating dust of an empty room, naked, white-walled, soulless.

Wolf

So I screw the lock back to the door. Just as well there's no cameras or alarms.

"I'm off!" I yell. "Give the door a hard slam when you leave, will ya?"

She doesn't hear. She's standing still as a statue. Then she disappears into a room. So I step into the hallway, close the front door behind me. The Vines. Never thought I'd get to see the inside.

Seven break-ins and I weren't responsible for none of them, worse luck.

I tiptoe upstairs, so quiet even the mice can't hear us. Plenty of those about. Three bedrooms, which shall I choose? The smallest one said the baby bear. Perfect. Enough room to hide under the bed if necessary. The silence is wicked. I bounce on the bed. An uninterrupted night. No screws driving us crazy, no harsh lights in me eyes, no din going on outside me cage. Bliss.

Poppy

The mess on the floor. Blood on the walls. No, not blood, paint. Spots of vermillion as though Mum had been experimenting. One of her wacky pieces, paint splattered over canvas. I try to explain this to the police-lady but she just strokes my shoulder. I push her away. Mum's high heeled stiletto is lying on the rug but she won't let me pick it up. There's a note. No, no note, so why do I think there was a note? Perhaps Cliff will remember. Cliff. I was supposed to call.

Poppy and Cliff

"I'm here, Cliff. I'm standing in the living room."

"How do you feel?"

"Empty. Emotionless."

"Are you on your own?"

"I'm trying to think back to how life was before. But it's as though my life before that day didn't exist."

"Lucky you."

"Cliff, you didn't come home for ages that day. You weren't at school. Where were you?"

"I went through it all with the police. Many times."

"I never believed your story about rescuing a sick dog, even if they did. Where were you, really?"

"None of it matters now."

"Do I remember you saying something about a note, or am I imagining it?"

"Poppy, just don't go there, ok."

"I need to know!"

"Ok, just keep this to yourself. Promise. You're dead right, I didn't go into school. I hated school. I was down the park with some mates, smoking dope. I came home lunchtime. Didn't expect Mum and Dad to be in, they were meant to be setting up an exhibition in Birmingham or somewhere, but I heard them in the living room, bickering. There were bags of shopping everywhere. I didn't stay long enough to find out what was going on. I sneaked into the kitchen to get some food and saw it on the kitchen table. Addressed to us."

"The note? Addressed to us both?"

"I stuffed it into my pocket to read later. I assumed they'd changed their plans and were having one of their dos. Remember their parties? No, you wouldn't. We were always banished to our rooms."

"I don't know if I can take this. I came here to try to remember what it's like to be part of a normal family."

"Normal family?"

"You have family. I have nothing. No-one."

"We were never a normal family, Pops. Mum and Dad only cared about showing off that house, showing off their extravagant possessions, showing off Mum's stupid 'artworks', showing us off until we became an embarrassment to them."

"I don't want to hear this."

"They were up to their eyes in debt yet they kept spending, going off on exotic holidays, throwing lavish parties. Selfish bastards."

"Mum and dad were murdered for goodness sake! How can you say those things?"

"Look… Katie's calling now. Must go."

"You were telling me about the note."

"It's nothing to worry your head about now."

"Do the police know?"

"No. No need."

"But it might throw some light on why that thug did it."

"If he did it."

"Of course he did."

"It was The Vines that killed them. It was greed."

"Just scan the note and send it to me, can you?"

"Sure."

Poppy

Warped panes of glass in the French doors distort the world outside. The back garden. Dad's pride and joy. There were cherry trees, apple trees, laburnum. There were grapevines. Dad would make his own wine and we were allowed to sample it. He dug a pond, filled it with water-lilies. He built a swing seat for Mum with his own bare hands. I can see it now, I can hear their laughter, even though I can't recall their faces. My big brother is wrong. We were a happy family. Cliff was the one with problems.

Dead flies fall as I pull back the velvet curtains, turn the rusty key, push open the doors and step outside.

Leaves dance around in the descending dusk but they are not from this garden. This garden is bare. Just withered grass and mud stretching to the back fence. Then I remember; squads of police out there for weeks, digging, pulling everything up, the fruit trees, shrubs, vines. Even the terrace. Searching for Mum and Dad's bodies but failing to find them.

The Vines

She prowls around the grounds like a lost cat. Once she would gather daisies, build tree-houses, fill them with families of dolls. Then her brother would knock them down and there would be tears. Ah, the days when the garden boasted greenery, when it was a welcoming home for its winged and four-legged inhabitants. Now they seek refuge indoors.

The fellow in the bed upstairs stirs, picks up his bottle to take a swig, curses when he finds it empty. He gets out of bed, fumbles for the light switch, stumbles around the room, tapping the walls.

Wolf

Time to explore, me thinks. I pull on me trousers, she'll be long gone but you never know.

So I check under the bed, the floorboards, nothing. No sign of any hidden safe. There's a cheap chest-of-drawers. Empty. Not the kind of furniture you'd expect in a grand town house. Suppose it's been rented out. Students or the like. So many of these places are these days. Bad for business. I remind meself, I'm going straight. Least that's what I promised. Right, let's try the other rooms.

So here we have the master bedroom. Wardrobe infested with wood lice. An old sock, poof! Nothing else. Then it comes to me what Jonno told us. The Vines was a doddle to break into. Every burglar's dream. Amateur security devices, wads of cash stowed in obvious places. Yet, bizarrely the real murderer left everything untouched. We'd joke about it during exercise hour. Whichever of us got out first would get in there and clean out whatever they left behind.

Poppy

Vines cover most of the windows at the back, twisting and turning around the hotchpotch of rooms, reaching up as far as the attic. When we moved here Cliff and I fought over who would sleep up there until Mum bagged it for her studio. I can picture her canvases in their lurid clashing colours, smell the pungent aroma of paint and alcohol. Half empty glasses of wine, half eaten sandwiches, cigarette stubs lying everywhere. Not everyone understood her work back then. So sought after now though. I should have kept more. At least the paintings I sold enabled me to buy my own place. The irony is that no-one was interested in buying them when she was alive. As with all great artists.

Our bedrooms occupied the floor below. Mine between Mum and Dad's room and Cliff's. Like being in a sandwich between Cliff's deafening music and Dad shouting at him to turn it off.

But something strange is happening. Am I imagining it or are the bedroom lights coming on, one by one? Is someone moving inside the rooms or are the trembling leaves creating an illusion?

Cliff

I start to type. To explain about the note. I still don't know what to make of it, even after all these years.

Poppy, I don't know if your visit jolted memories. Maybe best if it didn't. You see, there's more…

No. Can't say that. Not with her in that fragile frame of mind.

So, Poppy, I was going send a photo of the note but the writing has faded.

On the other hand, maybe she should know. She'll just have to deal with it, like I had to.

Pop's, Here's what the note said. Draw your own conclusions: 'My precious children....'

But as I type and see the words in print, I realise how much trouble I could get into. For withholding a piece of evidence. The repercussions. The case being re-opened. Especially in light of the appeal. My reputation ruined, just when the business is starting to take off. Wish I'd never mentioned the damned note. But then you never need to know the truth, do you? So instead I type:

Hey Pops, hope you got home safely. Hope the trip helped. Sorry I couldn't make it. Oh and that note I mentioned. It was nothing. Just instructions for our supper. I thought you might like to see it as it's the last thing Mum wrote. I'll show it to you when I see you. If I remember where I put it, that is.

I press send then I smile to myself. At least it was partially true.

Poppy and Wolf

"What are you doing in my parents' bedroom?"

"Was your parents' bedroom. Ain't now. Ain't even your house."

"I'm calling the police."

"And telling them what? You assisted me breaking and entering remember."

"You tricked me..."

"And you was lying to the agent about wanting to purchase this place."

"That's none of your business. If I'd have realised you were a filthy down-and-out I would never have bought you a drink."

"Exactly. That's what your lot are like. That's why we rob you. We despise you."

"Rob us?"

"I've been inside love, if you haven't guessed. In and out umpteen times. House-breaking is my trade, jail my home from home. I know all about this place. The stories that circulated. Knew the chap who never done it too. Jonno."

"Don't ever mention that name to me."

"Jonno is innocent. He's appealing, ain't you heard?"

"Innocent? He'd already robbed us twice. Can you even begin to imagine what that feels like?"

"Jonno is nothing more than a petty thief. What's more he respects his victims. He detests violence. Wouldn't get involved in any of the fights back in the nick. Jonno the gentle giant we called him."

"So how do you explain the call my Mum made as she lay dying? She had the presence of mind to describe her attacker down to the tattoos on his chest that matched his."

"And how do you explain why he didn't want the reward money for disclosing where their bodies were? Think he knew? Naah. Just a clever framing job."

"Framed? Who would do that? Why?"

"Plenty of theories going round the nick. Most popular one is it was someone in the family."

"You never knew our family. You have no idea what we were like. My parents were respectable people. Dad a brilliant businessman, Mum so beautiful, so talented, always surrounded by admirers. I can see them now…"

She starts to laugh. Her shrill laughter echoing through the empty rooms.

"I can see them! I can remember their faces. Exuberant, sparkling, grinning at each other. Always in love. Till the day they…."

Her laughter changes to hysterical sobs.

"We were the problem. We were always in the way. They wanted to live life to the full, without the burden of annoying, disobedient children. Not that they were bad parents, just... disinterested. We took advantage, did what we liked..."

Her sobs become uncontrollable, her body shaking, convulsing, howling; the pitiful cries of a lost child.

Wolf

Know just how she feels. Abandoned. Misunderstood. Angry. Story of me childhood. Part of me wants to give her a big hug, comfort her. But that would certainly land me in trouble. So I offer her a glass of something strong, if I can find a glass that is. Kitchen cupboards all bare. So I rinse out me empty vodka bottle, fill it with rusty tap-water tell her to pretend it's the real thing. Her tears are drying up now. She attempts a smile. Asks me what I do for a living. Apart from housebreaking. Garden maintenance I tell her. Odd jobs and the like. If she ever needs a handyman she should get in touch, I say. She takes my number. She has a big house, you can always tell. Massive, brimming with... naah. Going straight, this time. Definitely.

I decide not to tell her the other theories that were circulating. It's like MI5 in the nick. We may not be allowed mobiles or our own computers but there's a network of gossip, a steady stream of information that the screws never ever get their filthy rotten hands on.

Poppy

I check my phone. No more messages from Cliff. No more excuses, ah but there's an email. He says the note was just instructions for our dinner. How stupid does he think I am?

Suddenly its caving in on me. This house. Its tangle of vines like claws around my neck. All I want is to get out into the night air. I tell the convict he can squat inside if he wants. I won't tell anyone. He says he'd rather not. I suspect the place is giving him the creeps too. Part of me feels sorry for him, I doubt he has anywhere to go. I contemplate offering him my spare room in return for all the odd jobs that need doing, but I don't.

Cliff

I get down the box that I keep on top of the wardrobe, rummage though old letters, bank statements, faded photos from my youth; my class at school, my gap year in Venezuela.

Ah, here it is; the note. Mum's scrawly handwriting on the envelope, smudged and fading: *Poppy and Cliff*. I scrunch it up in my hand, take it to the back of the garden, place it on some decaying compost and light a match.

I don't know how long I've been standing here watching the flames when I hear Katy's frightened voice behind me asking what I'm doing. "Building a bonfire," I say.

"Is it bonfire night then?" she asks.

I put my arm around her shoulder and lead her back inside. "Nearly," I tell her. "We'll have a big family bonfire party, you me and Mum. What do you say?"

Dawn and Dom

Dawn stands facing the beach and adjusts her easel. She dips a brush into Prussian blue acrylic and follows the rise and fall of a wave crashing on to the rocks. Then she dabs yellow ochre curls on the head of a woman sitting on a dune, and, picking up a finer brush, adds streaks of silver grey.

Dom pours two cocktails, takes one over to Dawn.

"What do you think?" She asks him.

"Nice. Though I prefer your whackier stuff, the hot colours, eccentric shapes."

"I can't risk doing that kind of thing now. I'm a 'dead artist,' remember."

"The woman on the beach looks out of place dressed in winter clothes."

"English summer. I'm trying to decide what colour her hair is now. I hope it's not still that mousy blonde. Red would suit her."

"Put her out of your mind, Dawn."

"I wonder if we have grandchildren yet? I could paint them playing on the sand."

"Ok," He adds a scoopful of ice to his drink, takes a gulp. "Cliff has a daughter. Poppy lives alone."

"We promised each other never to try to find out. So how..."

"And you promised never to talk about them again."

"When I put them into a painting, it helps. Somehow it makes me feel as though I'm keeping up with their lives; imagining where they are, what they're up to."

"Why don't you look them up on Facebook, spy on them that way?"

"Too tempting to get in touch."

"Don't you ever even consider it babe. It would be more than our life is worth."

Dawn takes a long sip of her drink, stares at the wild Southern Ocean.

"Dom, there's something I could never bring myself to tell you. The day we left, I wrote Poppy and Cliff a note."

"You did what?"

"I didn't say anything that would give our plan away, just told them how much I would miss them. That I would always love them no matter what happened. I knew it was a risk…"

"That's an understatement. So what else did you say?"

"Nothing. Well, just not to believe everything they would hear. I apologised for being a bad Mum, said I'd stocked up the cupboards with enough food to last…"

Dom crashes his glass down so hard that it cracks, leaking a puddle of fizzy cocktail on to the patio table.

"Christ! If that ever gets into the wrong hands…"

"It would have done by now. We ruined their childhood, Dom."

"We did them a favour. They'll never need worry about paying off our debts. And the cash they received from your paintings means they'll always be financially secure."

"That's some comfort. Sure. But as time goes on, I find the guilt harder to deal with. And every time I see the scar on my arm I think about that poor chap serving a life sentence for our 'murder.'"

"Every time I look at my scar I think what a good job you did. You almost killed me."

"Accidentally."

"You deserve an Oscar for that performance you put on down the phone."

He attempts a choking sound, mimics her strangulated screech, "Help we're being attacked! I've been knifed. The blood won't stop…."

"Stop it, Dom. He doesn't deserve it."

"He deserves it for the times he broke into our home, the disgusting mess he made, remember?"

"We're alright now, aren't we? Everything's paid off, isn't it?"

"Sure. Nothing to worry about. Ever again."

"I wonder who lives in The Vines now?"

"No-one. They can't sell it. I believe it was rented out to students for a while."

"How do you know all this?"

"Don't ask."

Dawn moves back to her easel, picks up a brush. Dom tugs at her robe which slips off her shoulder. He kisses her tanned back.

"I'm going for another swim, babe. The sea is glorious today. Coming?"

The Vines

A blast of winter air blows in as my ex-inhabitant opens the front door. A flurry of dead leaves dance into the hallway, a stray cat slips past unnoticed and shoots upstairs.

My visitors step into the night, close the front door behind them, stand on the stone steps chatting for several moments. She hails a passing cab, gets in, waves to him. He starts to saunter slowly along the street. As her cab pulls away, she winds down the window, shouts out:

"Need a lift?"

He hesitates for a moment then climbs into the cab beside her.

Floorboards creak, pipes in the walls groan. The intruding cat jumps on to a bed, curling and mewing. Moths feast on threadbare carpets. Spiders weave webs, bats play in the attic, ghosts drift through ceilings. This house is never unoccupied, never empty. Only its secrets remain silent, forever trapped within these walls.

Dave's Vigil

1

For two days Dave has been sitting at the kitchen table as if he could still see her preparing her foods. The smell of white wine lingers, though he has cleaned the floor. The Sauterne leaves a rancid smell penetrating deep inside his queasy stomach. He jumps at the sound of the refrigerator motor grinding away. When he hears a car slow down in front of the house, he stands up and peeks out hoping to see the Volvo parked outside. He imagines the garage door opening and closing but then there is an absence of her rushing up the steps and the opening of the apartment door. He hears the sound of rain and he worries that she is cold. He opens the hall closet and sees her red raincoat hanging next to a black fleece. He wonders where she might be. Then he feels hate - hate at his predicament.

It's lousy, what I feel inside. I hate my stories, rattling around in my mind, relentlessly. I hate emotional songs - the ones that pull for loneliness. I hate being alone. I'm afraid to be alone. I hate it more than anything. So cold I am. My fingertips and toes. So stiff I can't bend them. I don't want to get up because I hate the cold floor and the dark nights, so I just lay in bed bending my knees, holding my body for warmth, hoping it will spread to my fingers, my toes. But I miss her smell and the way she rested her hand on her cheek while she slept. I liked to stare at her, mimic her inhalations and exhalations. They help me to sleep. I loved her long eyelashes and her silky hair. I smelled it while she slept. No Kidding! I'd wrap a piece of it around my finger. You think I'm a wimp. I bet you do. Long after she fell asleep I just stare at her.

I kick myself for what I did to her. My problem is my impulsive nature. The way I act on my thoughts. She used to like that when we were dating. I used to surprise her, come to her when she wasn't expecting me, bring a second bike, take her to the wine country on a surprise tour of the vineyards. I liked to surprise her but this one - me and one woman, then another - shocked her.

I'm alone. I watch the clock. It never moves, same as with my job; since we lost our market in Europe selling prunes I stay around the dark office. Who the hell loves prunes anymore? I hate my boss, too. He plays elevator music all day. That's the music I hate. He plays Ray Conniff, Jr. - I say tomato and you say toe-mah-toe, I say potato and you say pa-tah-toe, tomato - to-mah-toe. All day long that simple shit song drives me nuts. It's like counting my toes over and over again. The guy sings these simple-ass songs all day long. And I drive a long way to get to work in San Jose and I don't want to know the way to San Jose, that god-awful city. Now when I get home she's gone. I'm glued to the house, hoping the door will open, but it stays shut.

If I could just get a glimpse of her. That's it. I could explain it better. I must have said it wrong. Explaining myself is not my best skill. What is my best skill? I don't have one. I'm a sham. She doesn't want to see me. I can't leave. She'll come back. She won't come back. She loves me, she loves me not, a game I used to play as a child. The last petal, she loves me not.

What's that about why she didn't she leave a sap like me sooner? I'm no good. It'll go on forever. If I rocked the boat, it would be the thing that made her leave or....made her stay. So I didn't say anything. She found the crappy note on my cell. "Meet me at Di Vino, Maggie." Make no waves, Dave, I tell myself. I'm No-Wave Dave. Just think I went from being impulsive Dave to No-Wave Dave. In a second. A switchman!

Oh Jesus is there another way? A hot or cold guy, is that it? Shit or get off the pot, Dave. That's what my mother used to say to my father, "Shit or get off the pot, Dave". He was Big Dave. Well he sure did get off the pot and flew the coop.

I'm afraid of my shadow. I was stuck to my mother after my brother died and my father left and took my big sister. Afraid that if I didn't tend to her in a certain way, she'd leave too. Now I'm afraid to make a move, stuck to myself. Cocky and sloppy. I deserve to be alone, the creep that I am. No, I at least need to call Maria.

He picks up the phone. "Hi Maria, it's Dave, have you seen her?"

"Sorry, Dave," Lina's sous chef says.

"She hasn't contacted you? Are you sure?"

Then he inquiries of the Franks, Lina's clients. Then he calls her friends, Cheryl and Tim. Nothing! They haven't seen her. He looks at his wristwatch, it's almost noon. He has a few minutes before her taiji class is over. *If she's still in SF, she'll certainly be at Golden Gate Park doing taiji. Now I'm going to miss her. Asshole! Why the hell didn't you think about this an hour ago!* He hops on his bike, forgetting his helmet. He heads down 36th Avenue, crossing Anza, Balboa, Cabrillo, and Fulton on into the park, feeling dense moisture on his ears. He squints at the fog as if it will help him see more clearly.

He stops at Spreckles Lake where a group of twenty students sway their arms, moving like snakes or rambling bears. At the lake's edge, they follow their teacher, an older man who stands facing them. He never got why Lina liked this kind of movement. *Not for me.*

Looking at each one slowly, Dave immediately knows she's not there. If she were there, he would feel that magnetism rising in him. Yet he still looks at each one's face in false hope. Stopping in front of a bench he watches a male student with a ponytail and loose fitting pants. Dave wonders about his hair and the strange dance he does. Seems to him that this sport is for sissies. It never really occurred to him to ask Lina what it was - this taiji. He doesn't really know what they're doing and feels a little odd hanging around staring at them, but they seem not to notice him. As he gets to the third row he recognizes Lina's friend Kata who seems to be in deep focus with her eyes gently closed and her facial muscles soft. He watches her arms move like the branches of the pine swaying in the wind. He sits on the bench mesmerized by the flow of the dance, daring to feel a glimmer of hope. He waits for her to notice him. She sees him, but doesn't make a move toward him. He keeps his eyes on the woman with the soft white hair, the rosy cheeks, and the dancing arms. When the class breaks, he makes a move toward her. He wants to make sure someone else doesn't get her attention. He fears she'll rush away when the class breaks and he'll miss out.

"Where is she?" he says. The woman looks, doesn't answer. "Hello," he tries again, "Kata?" The woman looks up. He says, "Lina left two days ago and I'm concerned she's missing. Has she contacted you?"

The woman remains silent. He wonders if she's in some altered state.

"Oh, Hi Dave. She didn't come here yesterday either. I thought maybe she had a special dinner gig." Her gaze is blue and steady like a calm sea.

"I'm sick," he confides, "Can you help?"

"I'm sorry," she says. "You must have known this was coming on, it was just a matter of time," she says. Then she turns away.

"Damn!" he says, knowing that Kata and whoever else in this sissy crowd have been talking about his life. To hell with them. He jumps on his bike and heads out toward the beach, along JFK Drive past the buffalo fields and toward the windmill close to Ocean Beach, hoping he will see her Volvo. It's very quiet when he arrives at the great stretch of shoreline where she sometimes ran. It's damp and foggy, making for poor visibility. Squinting does nada. He pulls out his cell, dialing the number he's dialed dozens of time since Lina left. Always the same voice, the same story, "Leave a message for Cheryl or Tim." He throws the phone into the bike bag. Then retrieves it immediately and dials her clients, remembering Kata's words, "maybe a dinner gig." He's hoping that he'll find her there cooking for this evening so he dials their number again. Mr. Frank answers.

"We're wondering where she is, too, Dave. I hope she hasn't had an accident," he says.

"An accident? I hadn't thought of that! Oh, my God. What if she's lying in some hospital injured!" He hangs up the phone. What have I done to her! Knots grip him as he replays his childhood.

His dad is holding him. Dave's body convulses. They are both crying.

"It was an accident, son. You didn't do this intentionally," Daddy says, "it was my fault."

How could I be so out of touch? How come I didn't think of this? It's all my goddamned fault. The same old thing, my fault. Mea culpa. The whole thing right from the start, he says to himself, recalling his dad trying to convince him he didn't do what he did. He calls the Richmond District police station and connects with missing persons. Officer Ryan asks some questions and then reads him the protocol for filing missing persons request. He hangs up and proceeds down the beach, knowing that she is indeed missing, but not kidnapped. If anything she is free from him, maybe even glad to be rid of him.

For the first time he's angry at the Franks for all their requirements on Lina, "Those elitist snobs can't even cook for themselves. Fussy bastards. Demanding sustainable organic produce and meats," he says to no one. "Who the hell do they think they are? Doesn't their shit smell, too?" For a moment he's thrilled that Lina left them hanging. He could imagine Mrs. Frank with her pert little nose and her thin lips quivering when she found a food cart, no food, and no chef. He wonders if she even knows how to boil an egg.

He lay down on the wet sand pounding his fists into the tiny rocks until he begins to feel the pain. He sees Lina's face, her dark eyes, her skinny body. "Damn her! Damn her, too! What a fool I've been. What a chump I am!" He sees himself pussy-footing around his own house, afraid to leave her all these years. Then an image of a little boy waiting for a crumb comes to him. The little boy is Dave, curly headed Davey with the liquid deer eyes. His daddy, inconsolable after the accident, leaves them. Dave feels a familiar cloud descend upon him, the one that has plagued him much of his life, the one that Lina managed to break through to reach him. He feels an ache that sometimes comes at night just as he's about to fall asleep. It seems to him a cruel ache that won't let him sleep. It starts inside his heart as a vague sensation that deepens until it feels like a gaping hole. The hole is round and deep and wants to eat something. He used to get up and eat a bowl of cereal, thinking he could feed the monster inside. But soon after he fell off to sleep he woke up again with the same gnawing feeling returned. He doesn't know what kind of food will soothe it. Voracious, it will devour him. He remembers a particular night after his dad left them when he had a fever.

He was eight years old and wore flannel pajamas. He slept alone after his brother was gone, slept in a single metal-framed bed in a room down the hall from his mother's. He woke up wet and hot in the partially darkened room. At first he thought that he had peed himself through his pajamas, but it was more like he was drenched all over. He tried to call to her, but he couldn't get the sound out, and the ceiling was moving back and forth and seemed to show him odd and scary faces with bulging eyes and grotesque wings. The house was quiet, but the ceiling seemed to be crashing in on him. He managed to pull himself out of his bed, the floor was stone cold and made him shiver. He crawled through the dark hallway into his mother's room. She was there asleep on her bed, an empty bottle rested in the bend of her arm. He pushed and prodded her to wake up.

"Mom, Mom, I'm scared. Their wings are big." Then the bottle came crashing to the floor. She woke up and looked at him.

"You," she said, "Get out of here." It was as if she was still looking for my little brother, as if she didn't know he was gone.

"Mommy," he kneeled at her bed and tried to climb in.

"Can't you let me sleep," she said turning away. He cried softly on the cold floor by the pieces of white glass and the wine until the morning.

Hot tears run down his fog-drenched face, seeming to make steam. The black hole grips him. He can't escape the gigantic mass of concrete and steel like the base of the Bay Bridge and he's sailing right into it. His sobs are craggy and rough-edged. His mouth wide open, his lips and jaws extended like the mask of tragedy. He wonders if he's inside his sobs. Then, he feels a light touch on his skin and wonders if he's redoing his dream. Maybe with a kinder mother comforting him. He opens his eyes to see a very little girl bent over him. He squints, unsure of what he sees. A pink rain slicker on a girl with a beach pail and shovel in her free hand.

"Crying," the girl says, bending closer to him. The tiniest finger tracing the stream of tears on his face. The child presses her fingers into his face, scratching him like she might her puppy. "Man crying, Mommy," she says again to someone else. He hears a woman's voice.

"Chiara, come here. Where have you been? Don't run away from me like that, especially in this fog!"

Dave watches the mother, so protective of her Chiara. He feels envy of the mother love.

"Mama, man crying," she points at the reclining man. The mother looks at his face. Then she says, "Chiara, don't bother the man. We have to go home now."

Dave sees her looking, and feels ashamed at his position, a man crying on the beach. He watches as Chiara takes her mother's hand. The mother looks back once more at Dave. "I'm sorry," she says. His eyes follow the two of them until they disappear into the fog. He doesn't want them to leave him. He gets up and rushes after them through the fog, following the child's voice. He can no longer see them so he runs and yells, "Please, Please, wait." He sees the pink slicker.

The woman stops. She is not so far away from him, it's just the fog that makes them invisible. She turns toward him, brushing her short blond hair from her eyes, as if she wants to see him more clearly. She takes an awkward pause, then says, "She's very sensitive and curious. I think she has radar for suffering. Sorry if she disturbed your...."

"Pain, Pain. My wife just left me and we never had a child." He didn't tell her that he'd lied to Lina. Never told Lina he'd had a vasectomy, let her think that infertility was her problem. The mother holds her child tightly to her breast. He feels envy for their bond. He tries to speak but his voice cracks. He coughs, catching his breath. He sees then that she's still standing there holding her child in her arms. Chiara is staring at him, her small hand at her lips as if she afraid of his sounds.

"I'm sorry." The mother says, turning away from him as if to go. Then she faces him as if she's just had a thought. "You know there's more than one way to father a child."

"More than one way to father a child," he repeats, staggering in the sand at her remark, dizzy, not really ever having thought that precise thought or knowing exactly what she means. He walks a step closer to hear her say, "Well, you've got to get over yourself first."

Her directness bites like sharp teeth in his soggy flesh. But then he realizes that she has responded honestly, at least she has taken a risk to say something to a stranger. He wishes that he had a friend to help him through this difficult time, even to confront him as she has, but then he hasn't been much of a friend to any one. The woman is still standing there. He wonders what she saw that provoked her to say what she said. He manages to respond. "Wait, please. Tell me what you see. I need a friend."

"Like I said, get over yourself." She pulls the child away.

"Bye, man," Chiara says. He watches them move toward the Cliff House where the fog is lifting. Then he retraces his steps through the fog to retrieve his bike. The gears are sandy. He decides to walk the twelve blocks to his house, crossing the Great Highway, walking up Balboa Street hill slowly, looking at the houses and the storefronts, stopping at the Sugar Bowl to buy a do-nut. The sugar tastes delicious and watery in his mouth.

After he rinses his bike, he goes up to his flat. The first thing he sees when he opens the door are her keys on the table. She had been there while he was out. He rushes to her room to see that her suitcase and carry-on bag are gone. He looks at the closet shoe bag and the empty spaces where her favorite t-strap shoes and boots had been. Shoes gone. He opens the panty draw - her black silk panties and bra are missing but the cotton ones are still there. He caresses the white ones. He looks at her make-up table - the cosmetics are missing - the red lipstick - the toothbrush. He sits on the floor by her bed and buries his head in her panties, smelling her, imagining his finger around a clump of her hair.

2

Dave bikes to the beach the next morning to see if he might find the woman and her child. No, they're not at the beach. He pushes uphill past Louis' restaurant where he finally feels free to breathe for the first time in three days. On inhalation he realizes he has been holding his breath. He decides to cross the Golden Gate Bridge north to Sausalito. The chill in the air announces the new season. With the wind biting at his face he pedals over the bridge where tourists hug themselves to keep warm. Instead of climbing Hawk Hill he pedals through Sausalito, passing the birdman with the white glove, holding the parrot for the tourists. How funny is memory? He thinks of Lina and their times in Sausalito. No he's not curious, it's more like he's finishing business. That thought makes him laugh. It's more like beginning business.

He looks across the channel where an icy white reflects off a fishing boat docked at the pier, sending shimmering light onto the water. Splotches of aqua blue, white and black dance, making an impressionistic painting. A few seagulls rest on moss covered rocks jutting out of the shallow water. Low tide? He really doesn't know much about the tides, and wonders if rowboats can dock safely in low tide. He sees the old man rowing. He envies him and he doesn't even know him.

On the next block he passes the movie theater, then the Sushi Ran, an upscale Japanese restaurant with a frog motif. The only frogs in there are the Prince Charmings, he thinks, who seem to be working their testosterone with the most beautiful women in the Bay Area.

He stops to get a look at people out for a Japanese brunch. Peering inside, he recalls having had dinner there with Lina on their first wedding anniversary five years ago when he was still her prince. As he stands before the glass he feels the excitement they had on their celebration. He salivates. He can almost taste her freshness, a combination of ripe watermelon and sage bud in his mouth.

He remembers Lina getting up from the table and running toward him as he entered, rushing to show him her new hairstyle. She loved him, then, and wanted him to touch her.

"You're so beautiful," Dave said.

"My celebration cut!" She twirled around, bouncing her head back to show him her stylish short-slicked hairstyle that accentuated her angular nose and long neck. "I'm so happy Dave. Our anniversary," she said, pecking his cheek. "Different, Huh? My mom had that long gray hair."

"For sure, you're breaking the habit," he joked.

She frowned at him, "Guess what Jake said today. He told me that with my business sense he sees the company going public. Do you know what that means, Dave?"

"You'll be a CEO?"

"I don't know about that, but we'll have money to travel and I'll have a résumé."

"Fantastic, what more could a guy like me want, a beautiful wife with a new hairstyle, a great job, and the best fuck," he said. She snuck a little nibble at his upper lip.

"You know I finally feel acknowledged. I never quite understood trust until you," she pecks him again. Dave shivers in his skin. He's a dumb fuck - never told her about the accident when he was eight or the subsequent decision to never have children. He left that out.

"Amazing!" All he can say.

"Let's talk about my own endowment, you." She bends into him.

"You're pretty well endowed as you are," he said, touching her thigh lightly, "I love you, Lina. Kiss me hard." And she did.

He stands at the window his lips almost pressing into the pane, seeing not only her great beauty and talent, but also the little kids she planned on having.

"Twins, one for each boob," she'd say. He and she had even found names for the boy and girl they might have had - Molly and Max Randall - if he weren't such an asshole; worse, a liar. Since she went off the pill she was already checking into a preschool in Laurel Heights. She figured that she'd have their babies after her company went public so that her shares would be valuable. He loved how she experimented with living her life, so energetically, but also she pulled him toward his very best. How had he betrayed his best friend? His lover? His own future?

Since then he and Lina seemed to be living in their own separate cages in one big cage, their home. The cage has a concrete floor in which his feet are stuck. He hates it. He already felt lonesome. A dark feeling crept up on him, taking hold of his insides as he watched her tears puddle on the tabletop. Her sobs loud, at first, petered out into a vibrating hum. He listened to her weeping song, feeling his own ache between his shoulders. His came as a sharp zigzagging pain between his shoulder blades. With her leaving he understood for the first time how someone could have her heart break. A door had shut on him.

He hears tapping. Then he sees people at a table inside the restaurant, a man and a woman rapping their forks on the window, laughing at him. They're motioning for him to go away. He then sees the large chef's special, a platter of delicately carved and scooped raw fish on little clouds of rice. Orange flesh of salmon sat next to yellow tail, a dollop of wasabi, the rosebud ginger, all created a rainbow of beauty. Rainbows are made of sun and tears. He gently bows, as a way of excusing his daydreaming at their window seat.

3

For the next few days Dave skips work. After praying for Lina, he feels lonely and can only think of the never-existent children they had. Where had his treasure gone? He returns to the beach in hope of finding the mother and child, repeating in his head the mother's words, *get over yourself*. He retraces his steps. Everyone who approaches him resembles the pair. Has it always been that the beach was filled with mothers and children? He wonders why he's never noticed all these children, playing with dogs and balls. When a ball comes his way he instinctively positions himself so that he volleys it right toward a boy who produces an enormous smile as he then hits it perfectly to another boy.

When the boys finish laughing they rush toward Dave and ask him to show them how he did that. Soon he's teaching them to follow the ball and to work with its energy. He feels content when one of the boys connects with the ball. It's as if he's helping in some meaningful way.

"Will you show me?" says the smallest boy. "I want to do that, too."

The boy runs toward an older man wearing a suit and tie and dress shoes. "Dad, I just volleyed a ball," he says, looking toward Dave and jumping with an enormous smile. The man in the suit looks toward Dave.

"Can you show him?"

"Me?" Dave says, looking behind him, feeling shy at the attention.

"Why not you?"

"Me for what?"

"Teaching these boys. Soccer practice," the man says. "No pressure," he says jingling some keys in his suit jacket.

"What do you have in mind?"

"Some afternoon games on the beach, if you have time," he puts out his hand then withdraws it. "Bill here," the man says.

"Dave." Dave's not sure what he next hears coming out of his mouth. "I have some time."

"Tomorrow, then. 3:15 to 4:30. Does that work for you?"

"Sure."

The next afternoon Bill shows up with four boys - a small group of kids to play soccer - Jimmy, Fred, Eric, and Jose. Dave wants the kids to have fun and to learn some of the basics, but mostly to learn how to live with the ball just as his Uncle Vince had taught him.

After the accident when he lost his little brother, Uncle Vince had taken time with Dave, teaching him soccer "It's the difference between a live and a dead touch," he said. "It's the first touch, Dave, that matters; the way you first meet the ball. Watch me." Then he demonstrated a standing-still first touch, which he called a dead touch, and then a moving first touch that keeps the ball dribbling. His Uncle danced with and around the ball. He was the one who had given him a home. He went to live with his Uncle Vince - he guessed he would have been the same age as Eric – nine, ten. Mom went into rehab, his old man disappeared, and Uncle Vince played ball with him every day after school, both basketball and soccer in the park near the house in the Sunset District, not so very far from here. Then when Mom came home, the practice stopped. Her drinking and his care-taking began all over again. She'd called him her little man, which meant he was supposed to take care of her, but she never forgave him. Dave remembers overhearing her talking to her one friend Marge when she returned from the rehab.

"The worst thing about losing my son was losing my dreams. Dreams I had for Spencer like what would he be? A musician, he liked to play guitar; a dancer, the way be bounced around the house so playfully; a teacher, the way he explained things to his older brother, imagine; a cyclist, the way he popped wheelies as a kid and now the Stump jumper. A father, a husband, a graduate student?

"I died with him," she said.

Bill, Eric's father, interrupts him. "You know, Eric's having a breakthrough with that ball. It's that thing you said about bringing the ball into the house and moving it around with you. I'm no longer irritated with him about playing inside. Would you consider a Saturday practice at our house. We have a little park across the street?" asks Bill.

Dave feels like a piece of crap. An imposter. Can't he see it? And now he's asking me to teach his kid about love. If he only knew. Dave's stomach mashes inside him.

They stand away from each other, watching the kids. Fred's ball slices toward Eric who slams the incoming ball with the outside of his thigh but far from his buddy so that the ball pounds into the surf.

He watches the kid run into the surf with his below-the-hip jeans, so determined to retrieve the failed volley. Just out of reach of the ball the boy plunges forward into the surf, his pants dropping with the weight of the water. Blindsided by an incoming wave, the boy disappears into the crashing tide. Without a second thought Dave runs in after him. The wave has turned and he can see the boy in its curl. Adrenaline surges through him as he dives in and swims toward the boy who is wrapped in a second curling wave. Focusing on the spot where he last saw the boy go down, Dave swims under and grabs him. Together they ride the next wave toward the beach. The boy clings to him like a heavy weight as they scuffle and thrash into the surf where Bill's outreached hands pull them safely onto the beach. A small crowd gathers with Jose, Fred, and Jimmy. Eric collapses on the sand coughing, but okay.

"That was some surfing, Eric," Fred says.

"You should have seen that wave. It took you down man," says Jose.

"Wish it could a been me," says Jimmy.

"And look at your pants, Dad," says Eric laughing, "they're down around your butt like ours."

"That confirms what I was asking Coach Dave just before the tidal shot. We'll have our practice in the park across from our house from now on. Now that we have some thigh dribblers in this crowd."

"Here's my cell number." He hands Dave a card.

Dave agrees to rearrange his work schedule so that he works in the mornings and the evenings, leaving the late after school hours free for playing ball with the kids. Alert and awake now, he thinks of Chiara's mother wondering, *would she think I'm over myself?*

4

Dave hasn't looked at the mail in three weeks. He brings it up through the basement in the plastic laundry basket and dumps it untouched in the center of the round table in the kitchen where he hasn't eaten a meal since the coquille crashed to the floor. He prefers eating his take-out in the car or on the sofa in front of the TV. A large manila envelope slides off the table. It's addressed to Lina, sent priority from the Ahwanee Hotel in Yosemite National Park. He startles at the letterhead, knowing Lina had applied for the chef's winter program for 2006, that would be in a few months. He thinks of opening it, hoping to deem her whereabouts. He flips it over, handles it carefully as if its contents might come alive. He feels a pulsing though his body at the possibility of discovering her hideout. He imagines her excitement at receiving this parcel. He pictures her dancing about on her toes, waving the envelope. When she finally settled down she'd press her lips together holding her breath as she sliced through the paper with the kitchen knife.

He dials the answering machine for Cheryl and Tim, remembering the number by heart, having dialed it almost daily since she left almost three weeks now. He's in a sweat. What if she's there and she answers? No way is she waiting for him to call, even if she is hiding there. If she isn't, he knows they are in touch. She has to have had help. They are the help.

When Cheryl answers, he's taken aback.

"Hello. Who is it?"

"Dave."

"Oh."

"How is she?" No response. "Don't worry I plan to give her space," he says.

"Do you have a choice?" Cheryl says.

Biting his tongue, ignoring her sarcasm, he says, "Please pass a message onto her. Tell her it looks like she has an invitation from Yosemite to participate in the chef's week this winter at the Ahwahnee Hotel."

"Oh."

Dave hangs up the phone, tired of the Oh, Oh, Oh's from Cheryl's prissy lips. He feels heat rising around his neck. This God-darn flannel shirt is for the birds, he pulls at the collar to get some air. He's shut out from the loop of his wife and her friends. Then he's envious of her for having friends that protect her. He realizes that he hasn't any real friends. Lina is his best friend and he has betrayed her. He's at ground zero now, needing to begin again. The phone rings, making him jump. What if it's Lina? What will I say? I killed a boy and that's why I won't have kids. His hands shake. He picks up.

"Hi, it's Cheryl. I just wanted to say that Lina is okay. I've spoken to her. She's in India."

"India! She hates Indian food!" He can't move. He can't believe what he's just heard. *How in hell did she get there? She never wanted to travel with me to France to visit the vineyards. What is she doing cooking tofu?*

"Well, that's all I wanted to say. She wanted me to tell you she's okay and for you not to worry. I'll get the message to her. Now goodbye, Dave."

"Wait Cheryl. Tell her not to give up on me. Tell her that I'm working on getting over myself." He hears her on the line. She hasn't hung up on him. "Cheryl, thank you for telling me where she is. I've been awfully worried."

When she hangs up he loiters around in the hallway with his thoughts. *Maybe she's taking yoga classes. Isn't that something like taiji? I'm so dumb. I don't even know what the hell yoga is!*

Then he's in the hallway of his childhood home as a ten-year-old. He sees himself in striped overalls, his straight hair falls below his ears in a Beatle style cut. He's just come inside with his key to find his mother standing at her desk in the family study, her hands shaking. A cigarette rests in a ceramic turquoise fifties ashtray, which sits in a tall aluminum stand. Black block letters in the dish part spell Las Vegas. He knows she's proud of that purchase made when she was still single and working the Black Jack Table. She's dressed in gray slacks and a white nylon blouse, instead of her flannel pajamas. Her dirty smelly hair's pinned up with bobby pins, so that it's flat against her head, accentuating her bony features. Her lips are smeared with cherry red lipstick.

She comes at him pointing her stick fingers with the yellowed nicotine nail at him, "Why the hell do you blame others for what's your responsibility? You're the one that did it."

"Pammy, what?" he says, using the affectionate name she used to like.

"I hear you telling my family this and that. First it was my damn brother Vince you convinced I was unfit. Do you think I don't know, that I don't hear you complaining?"

"Pammy, Pammy. You'll get all excited and fall down again."

"Don't try to tell me. And don't you call me Pammy! I'm tired of all the stories about how I did this and I did that. You did it. You broke us apart, you little bastard." She picks up the turquoise ashtray, stand and all, and with one swift movement she swoops the stand up and over, smashing the brass base onto his head.

Red gushes over his face and eyes.

Before he faints and in a flash he sees the other red. Two boys, children, play with Daddy's 22 rifle, a barrel.

"Get the gun down. Let's play cowboy," the younger boy says. "You shoot me and I'll pretend DEAD."

The older boy with his hand on the metal, feels the coolness of the small rifle, puts his finger on the trigger, looks into the barrel. Bullet in there? Can't be. He doesn't see it or know how to check it, swivel it, turn it?

"No, go ahead. Stop looking for a bullet. I'll pretend," his brother says.

The resistance in the older boy's finger as he pulls the trigger and the trust on his little brother's face, comes to him as clear as day.

"Are you sure?" Dave asks.

"Go ahead. I'm okay, pull it. Do it."

"No, I'm scared," the older one says.

"Scared-y cat, pull that trigger."

"I'm not afraid," he says. Dave pulls and releases, feeling the push back.

"Boom!"

The boy falls.

Dave says, "Wow," shaking his hand out. "You can get up now." He walks over to his brother.

Blood oozing from his heart, puddles on the floor.

Pammy brings her hand to his head. She's saying, "Oh, baby doll, let me help you." She's dabbing the gash on his head with her nylon blouse. "Now, there, it's nothing, let your mama clean that up for you."

"You're not my mother," he says, "You don't act like a mother. You dumped me in exchange for your booze. You're sick!"

"Now baby don't say those things about the one that had you. There you go again with your stories, blaming me for all your troubles."

He's backing away toward the phone, dialing his Uncle Vince.

"How dare you, you ungrateful son of a bitch," she says, throwing the turquoise bowl at him, watching the ashes spill to the floor.

He moves toward the lit cigarette, crushing it under his Converse shoes.

The phone is ringing. For a moment he thinks it's the phone of his childhood, or that call from Uncle Vince telling him his mother died. He thinks about that day.

He reaches quickly for the phone. He listens as he holds it to his ear, feeling the ache in his heart for his brother and for Mama with her plastered hair and torn dreams.

"Hello," he says. He hears a woman's voice.

"Lina? Is that you calling from India?"

"No, Dave, It's Chiara's mother. I got your number from Bill on the beach."

"Excuse me'" he says.

"A few weeks ago we met on the beach. You were...."

"The man full of myself, yes, I remember. How's Chiara?"

"Well that's why I'm calling. I lost her."

"What?"

"Yes, in the fog. She got away from me like the day she found her way to you."

"What?" he asks, remembering her appearing as if through a cloud, bending toward him with her loving touch. His heart thumps inside his chest, announcing a panic at what he has just heard. "Is this a joke?"

"I wish it were. I'm devastated," she says. He wishes she'd speak louder.

"Excuse me," he says.

"The police are helping. Searching the beach. She wanders, you know," she says. "My only hope is that it's someone who knows her."

"How?"

"Well I can't be sure, but I think it's her father who took her to get back at me. We're in an ugly custody battle and he wants her too. I don't want to go accusing him if in fact he didn't take her. Just thought you might be of help."

He wonders if she wants him to lie around crying on the beach in the hope that she will come to him. "Really I don't see how I could be of help." I'm a killer, don't you know? Then he remembers the little girl bending over him with her fingers in his cheeks, her eyes searching his face, the little pail and shovel in her free hand. He is seized with sadness for her.

"Bill says you saved his son from drowning and I just figured... Mother's intuition... it's crazy. Sorry to bother you..."

"Wait! Wait! Where are you?"

"I'm at the beach walking near Lincoln."

"I'll be there in fifteen minutes. Wait. What's your name?"

"My name is Lisa" she says hanging up.

Dave receives the news, which cuts deeply. A child is missing, a beautiful sensitive, innocent girl. *Who am I to find her when no one else has managed? Lisa asks me not knowing that I caused a family, maybe two, to fall apart. Didn't I throw them down a rabbit hole?*

He pulls into a parking spot in front of a tall thin woman wrapped in a woolen coat-sweater with her arms clutching it in folds around her abdomen. When she sees him, she moves toward him arm outstretched. Her eyes look tired with red rims encircling her lids.

"Thank you for coming."

"I'm sorry about Chiara."

"I know she's alive. I know she's still here. I can feel her inside my heart, calling for me. Also I have a strong premonition that points me to you."

"You don't think I took her?" Where did that thought come from?

"No, I don't. I think rather that you can find her. I feel strongly that she has been kidnapped by her father and that she is at his place in the wine country."

"Can't you check that out?"

"The police have asked and every one is protecting him, saying he's out of town, unavailable. They've gone to the house, no response. They have no evidence to break in. I think she's at his place." She slows down. "What I need is for you to stake out the place, to watch their every movement. Listen for her voice. Are you interested in setting up camp nearby in the state park?"

"Why me?"

"You're a new face. Eddy won't recognize you and…" she pauses, "you need to do something to relieve your pain."

"What?'

"I recall how you want to father in some way, to protect a child, you know how you saved the boy from drowning. Here's your chance."

"You're giving me a gift then?" he says. Some gift alright, camping in a park somewhere.

"Yes, a chance to get over yourself." Her reddened eyes twinkle.

"When do I leave?'

"Right now, today."

"Right now? What about the four boys I coach?"

"Bill has agreed to set up dribble exercises with cones in the park."

"Okay. Tell me where I'm going."

Lisa looks around to see if there are eyes watching her.

"It's all in this envelope. The place is 55 miles North of the Golden Gate Bridge. A house on a dirt road on a hill. A big fence, wired at the park boundary, is the nearest point to the house. No dog! You can camp at the park nearby."

"How long?"

"Til you hear her voice."

He wondered about this commitment.

"Be my eyes, the eyes of a mother looking for her beloved."

"Yes, I'll put some things in order and leave after today's practice with the boys."

"Thank you, Dave. Here's my cell number."

They say goodbye.

5

After gathering a set of clothes, a sleeping bag, a tarp, and flashlight, he leaves town over the Golden Gate Bridge, heading North toward Sonoma. He reaches the road to the state park at dusk. Lisa's map shows a dirt road about a quarter mile from the entrance to the park. Once there he slows down at a wooden gate about five feet tall and a track beyond that leads to a secluded house. He passes the house and enters the park, a sign saying it closes at sunset. He drives past the ranger station and parks in a day lot, noting that there are no other visitors. He stashes his bag in a grove, taking a cross country path through the brush, making his way toward the house he had just passed; the shade from eucalyptus and oak make it difficult to see. He takes solace in the carpeted floor of pine needles and leaves, feeling every placement of his feet. When he comes to a circle of redwoods he makes a note to spend the night at its center where he will feel safe. About one hundred yards from the ring of trees, he sees a single light in the distance. On closer inspection it comes from a long ranch-style house. He stops, straining his eyes to get a sense of its configuration, suspecting that the kitchen is at the center of the sprawling home. Frightened by a squirrel jumping from one tree to another and the night sounds which surround him, he heads back to collect his belongings.

Once in the midst of the giant redwoods, he peers in what he thinks to be the direction of he house. As it grows dark his eyes slowly adjust. A light shines from the house; noises from the house are faint. At first he hears kitchen sounds, clanking utensils and dinnerware. Then he hears a child's sing-songy voice. The cadence, slightly musical and whiny, remind him of the soccer boys on the beach. *Likely a boy's voice, and not the flavor of Chiara's two-word sentences.* He hears her words on the beach, ones that he has repeated endlessly to himself. "Man crying," and "Bye, Man." *Not her*, so he decides to return to his sleeping bag. As he relaxes he hears an owl hooting and another off in the distance respond, *Hoo! Hoo!* The rise and fall of the dialogue lulls him to sleep.

"Waah, Waah, Waah, Waah," wakes him. *Was it the cry of a sheep or a goat?* But then he hears the rumbling tone of a man's voice responding to the distress. Dave gets up and moves closer to the wire fence boundary. The sounds grow louder. He sees a light in the side of the house away from the dirt road. In the curtainless window a shadowy figure hovers over something. The child continues to cry until finally reaching a place of heaving sobs. Then a quiet. The light goes out.

Was that her? Who was the figure hovering? A woman? The man he heard rumbling? Who was the boy?

Questions flood him as he falls into his bag and into a sleep. In a clearing he hadn't seen the night before, he sees the morning star pull up the sun. He sits up, wondering at the sight, small birds greeting the day. All of a sudden Dave is famished. He reaches for a Cliff Bar in his vest pocket. He sits savoring the peanut-buttery taste, licking his lips as the sun rises brighter in the sky. Among the crowing he distinctly hears a cry, "Want Mama, Want Mama, Want Mama."

That deep-hearted feeling he has begun to know creeps into his bag with him. His crying is also Chiara's. His soul screams with the little child calling for her Mama.

He gets to his car and calls Lisa, "I found her", he cries into the phone.

6

Dave jiggles the key into the lock and opens the door of his flat after his night's vigil at Jack London Park. He places the sack with his overnight gear on the floor and locks the door behind him. He's looking forward to a hot shower and then a nap.

"Hello, Dave," he hears Lina's voice and thinks he must be dreaming. Exhausted, he sighs then looks around the doorway into the kitchen. Lina is sitting at the round table. Her set of keys beside her ringless hand, which rests on the table.

He can't take his eyes off the keys. "But you left your set of keys!" He focuses on the day she took her bags and left her keys on the tabletop. "How'd you get in without keys?"

"Cheryl and Tim kept a spare for me."

"Oh! I'm confused. I just can't make sense... Is that really you?"

"Yes, I arrived home late last night."

"You did?" he says, still in disbelief.

"You weren't here. I know you don't like surprises."

He looked into her eyes.

"What I first loved about you was the way you looked into my eyes just like now. Then you stopped," she said.

"And then you hated me for it."

"Yes, I couldn't see you any more. It was like you were hiding." He wasn't sure he wanted to go here right now with her but she kept talking. "All the time you spent avoiding me. Keeping too busy figuring things, taxes, the bank accounts, the bills. I used to think you were doing that so you wouldn't have to look at me. Like they were more important than me. I was jealous of the time you spent away from me, then..."

"Someone had to do it," he says.

"Mostly, Dave, I wanted to see your eyes looking at me but you couldn't seem to meet my gaze."

"I know, Lina."

"I felt so lonely."

"Was that when you stopped talking to me?" he asks.

"Yes, maybe," she says.

He adjusts his gaze, bravely looking at her. "I thought you might see inside me, see how messed up I was." He jiggles the keys in his hand. "I stole looks at you when you weren't looking."

"I didn't know."

"I missed out. Your satiny brown eyes are so beautiful, they shine." He wanted to ask her if she were planning to live with him but he waited. "You're home, here with me at last from India. How was India?"

"India taught me a lot about myself."

"What?"

"First, I don't feel angry at you any more. I can't exactly explain it but it has something to do with India."

He sees her looking out the window at the rain. He remembers that it was raining the day she left, the first rain of the season he thinks. Was it a month, six weeks ago? So much has happened for him since then, and he imagines for her as well. He really can't get it that she's sitting beside him. Familiar. New.

"The softness of the rain," she says, looking out at the rain. He takes off his jacket and sits down at the round table. In silence they stare at the round drops that draw lines down the pane. Some of the drops hit the surface and then pull down until they evaporate or merge with another stream. He wonders if in their relationship the lines drawn between them are fluid or parallel, crossed or knotted. He doesn't know how that will look. Will he move out? Will he have her as a friend? Is she planning on leaving again? But more than that how can he show her that he has changed?

"I want to know why you couldn't look at me," she says. "The truth, Dave."

He grimaces with discomfort, leaning closer to her. She doesn't move away. The thought of their relationship evaporating like the raindrop disturbs him, causing his hands to tremble. He places one on the other. He looks toward her, wondering if she notices him. She has a soft look on her face, her facial muscles are relaxed, and her lips have a slightly upward curve.

"I have learned to love silence," she says. "Did you go silent after your brother died. Was it like this?" She looks at him, her eyebrows raised. He keeps his eyes on hers.

"No it was different. I think I was in a fog then. I sat for long periods with my head down so that my chin touched my chest, my hands tightly knit on my lap, with my knees bent, and my feet pulled close together. I had a small red cap that covered my eyes so I wouldn't see. I wore these gray fingerless gloves that my brother wore and just sat there holding my hands together. I just sat there."

"Oh, I'm sorry for the little boy you were," she says. "You never told me that before. I never asked about the details from that earlier painful time."

"And I merely pieced things together in a kind of brief feelingless summary, didn't I?" Dave says.

"I didn't know how to ask."

They sit together and listen to the rain. It's as if they're inside the rain in some protective bubble that he hopes won't burst. He knows his secrets are with them now because of the story he wants to tell.

"This silence is different, soothing and enlivening. Isn't it, Dave?"

"I was thinking something like that, too."

She smiles, then looks at him directly. "I'm sorry I was so rash with you and never really listened when you tried to explain. I just went off the handle. I never wanted to hear the truth," she says.

"You flew off the handle, and then you flew the coop."

"Coop it was," she says. "I'm not sure about us, Dave." She looks at him with questioning eyes. "I was so lonely here and I know nothing is certain."

He feels a pang. "I don't understand. Tell me."

"You and me. I want to trust it will all play out as it's supposed to. Organically! I've just come to see that some things are meant to be as they are. We are living them," she says.

"What do you mean?" He looks away. He feels her eyes burning into him.

"Dave, don't do that, Face me. Please look at me. Tell me."

"Lina, give me a chance, please.".

She backs off, gets up, and places a hand on his, moving him toward the living room and an overstuffed chair built for two, the one they bought in the small furniture store on Fillmore. They used to cuddle in it.

She sits down and pulls him to join her. He feels her fluidity as he accepts the pull. He's grateful and knows he can tell her now. Now is the time.

"Lina something awful happened when I was a boy."

She looks attentive, ready to hear him this time. He feels her thin shoulders and hips next to his, their legs and feet are side by side. She lets her loafers slip off onto the carpet while they sit quietly watching the rain through the picture window.

He says, "I killed my brother in a terrible accident. Shot him with my dad's rifle."

"Oh, my God!" she takes his hand.

"The awful thing is he died trusting me with the gun. Neither of us knew the thing was loaded. He died immediately. He trusted me and I shot him."

Lina slips her arms around his shoulders.

His upper lip quivers. His eyes fill. She tightens her hands around him. "Cry, Dave, cry," she says.

Retracting like a closed fist, he cries like a wounded animal. His body heaves. She holds him as the rain gently falls.

"My poor mother! She was all alone without her dreams."

"She wasn't there for you, Dave. You were alone too."

"I was desperately alone until I met you, Lina." They wrap themselves around each other on the overstuffed chair taking turns comforting each other.

"I'm so sorry Dave, for what you've lost."

He has to tell her about his infertility. He can't carry that another moment. "One more truth," he says. "You must know that I'm infertile. I had a vasectomy before I met you."

"Hummm," she says, a strange smile on her face. "I had a sense of it, Dave. Now I know why."

"Can you forgive me?"

"I do."

"Can I ever make it up to you, in some small way?"

"No, it's done. "

"I want to make up to you for what I've done," he says.

"How can we make up for the past? Let's live fully now."

"We'll see," he says. Her eyes light up.

"You know everyone in India says that," Lina says.

"I guess I've learned from your leaving me."

"What have you learned?"

"I've learned to get over myself. Tell me when I'm not looking into your dark and vibrant eyes. Please don't let me go away again."

"I'll keep in touch," she says, squeezing him.

"In what way?"

"We shall see," she says.

About the Authors

Nigel Ferrier Collins is a writer and visual artist whose articles, stories and poems have appeared in various newspapers, magazines and anthologies. He has MAs in English and American Literature from The University of Kent (thesis on Wallace Stevens), and in US philosophy and literature from Kings College London. He has been a detached youth worker, actor, special educational needs teacher, counselling trainer, education adviser, management consultant, and manager of a group of British international schools. He co-founded the Poetry Society at the University of Kent and arranged readings by many of the leading British poets of the mid sixties. He was involved with the early days of establishing the Old Fire Station arts centre in Oxford. He is the author of four books published by The National Youth Bureau (now the National Youth Agency), Heinemann Educational Books, and Oxford University Press.

Linda Davis' short story "The War at Home" won the *Saturday Evening Post* Great American Fiction contest. Other story and essay publications include *The Iowa Review*, *The Literary Review*, *Literal Latte*, *Gemini Magazine* and *Mothering Children with Special Needs*. She worked with Antonya Nelson at Bread Loaf, Robin Black at Lighthouse Lit Fest, and Francesca Lia Block at Antioch University where she received her MFA.

Linda is currently working on a collection of short stories titled *Echo & Narcissus* which depicts the psychology of a world divided between narcissists and those subjected to their exploitation. Readers get to be voyeurs, seeing a narcissistic character from the first story in an unforeseen dilemma, and in the second, its pair. *Devotion* and *Christian's Dab Bay* are one of seven pairs in the collection.

She lives in Santa Monica, California with her husband and three children.

Polly East is a north Londoner by upbringing and inclination who now lives in Brighton. Her early training in journalism and feature writing took her to Hollywood and the beginning of a lifelong connection with America. Later, back in the UK, she spent three decades raising a family and teaching English and Special Needs in challenging north London comprehensives, sporadically submitting poems and short stories along the way. Although writing since childhood, she did not often submit her poems to the stuffy scrutiny of the literary establishment.

Having had early minor successes and some interest expressed in her potential, she lacked the necessary commitment to keep plugging away at an elite cultural landscape where success was too often preordained and rarely a true reflection of creativity. Many years ago, she read with a small group - The Running Horse Readers - which aimed to go into prisons and old people's homes.

These days, she has more time and confidence to guide a few poems into the light; indeed, she was long-listed for the 2017 National Poetry Competition, and recently *Agenda* literary magazine put two of her poems into the Oxford Bodleian Library. She is currently a member of Brighton's Stanza group, and advocates that if something is good it will survive, finding its own place in our rich canon. She believes some of her poems will survive regardless. She feels she has not fulfilled her potential - but suspects that very few women ever do.

Ian Gouge is an author and poet who has published a number of novels, collections of short stories, volumes of poetry, and works of non-fiction. As the driving force behind Coverstory books, one of his aims is to help writers get their work seen by a wider readership (hence this volume and the two 2021 collections, *New Contexts*). Born on the south coast of England, Ian has travelled widely - including short stints living in Singapore, Switzerland, Grenada, and Sierra Leone. He now lives in North Yorkshire.

Denise McSheehy lives in Devon with her partner and two cats. She was educated in England and Northern Ireland and has an honours degree in English Literature. She received an Arts Council bursary and a grant from The Society of Authors towards work in progress. She has had two collections of poetry published, *Salt* (Poetry Can) and *The Plate Spinner* (Oversteps Books). Her work has appeared widely in various journals and anthologies, most recently *The SHOp An Anthology of Poetry*. She is currently working on a collection of short stories.

Carol Park roams from cities, to wilderness and cultural mazes. While teaching and befriending English learners from far places, she's realized how little she knows and how dear is tea and the meeting of minds.

Cultural intersections is her passion. Her marriage to a computer nerd from Hawaii — with grandparents from Korea — has given ample opportunities. What attracted provides conflict later — more than, *you like paper plates for company dinner? Ceramic is a must*. Deep sea diving for assumptions and neurological characteristics brings joy. Hence, six years spent in Japan. It brought beauty, change and precious friends. My daughters attended typical Japanese schools and, later, found spouses from non-western backgrounds. New foods — yay! Scouting for new manners — good!

Carol upped her writing through Seattle Pacific University's MFA program. You can enjoy photos of far places or read stories at CarolPark.us. Join her on Twitter @CarolPark2.

Her short fiction appears in *The East Bay Review, Harpoon Review, Shark Reef, Birdland Journal, The Raven's Perch, Red Wheelbarrow*, and the anthologies *Barbies that Were and Never Were*, and *Fault Zone: Strike Slip*. A novel set in Tokyo is forthcoming. Hear her at the Flash Fiction Forum of San Jose, CA.

Yvonne Sampson has had work shortlisted for many competitions, including the BBC Writersroom Prize, The Soho Theatre Westminster Prize, Exeter Writers Short Story Competition and The Write Festival Short Story Competition. The Write Festival short-listed stories were published in *The Short Story Competition Anthology* (6th Element Publishing).

A radio play she wrote won second prize in The Green Stories Writing Competition and her short fiction has won second prize in competitions run by Writers Weekend and Writing Magazine.

She recently had a story published in *New Contexts 2* (Coverstory Books).

Yvonne took an MA in Devising for Theatre at Kingston University and had plays showcased at The Rose Theatre Kingston and at The Etcetera Theatre as part of The Camden Festival. She has also written one-act plays which were performed at Stockwell Playhouse and The New End Theatre Hampstead for The Lost Theatre Company and at Watford Palace Theatre where she helped to set up and run a writers' group.

Yvonne worked as a drama teacher for many years and devised several plays with young people which were performed at youth drama festivals.

She lives in London and writes on a houseboat in Brighton.

Barbara Sapienza left her wild Sicilian family in Boston and drove to San Francisco in 1969 with a U Haul, a husband, and two babies She became a homemaker and a teacher surrounded by freethinkers.

Sapienza began writing twenty years later after earning a PhD and working as a clinical psychologist. Until then her stories were oral.

Her love of nearby giant redwoods, wildlife, San Francisco Bay, and the Pacific Ocean, all influence her abstract oil paintings and her writing. Sapienza's first novel, *Anchor Out*, features a woman who lives on the sea in Richardson Bay.

An alumna of SFSU's master program in creative writing, she is nourished by nature, meditation, tai chi, and dance. Her family, friends, and grandchildren are her teachers. She lives in Sausalito, CA with her husband and works on a memoir of life in her beloved Italian family.

Anchor Out (She Writes Press, 2017) IPPY Bronze, Best Regional Fiction, West Coast; *The Laundress*, (Kirkus Review, 2020) honorable mention; a forthcoming novel, Spring 2023. *An Ode to Gravity* shortlisted for *New Contexts: 2* (Coverstory Books). *Yellow Curry and Pink Bromeliads*, Read650; *Voices of Hope*, Carnegie Hall.

Recent publications from Coverstory books

Only Rumour Survives by David Smith

This eclectic collection sings with melancholy, humour, wistful reflection and evocative insight. Written in a concise style that makes for rare accessibility to inner meaning, this is a thought-provoking and original collection of poems.

David Smith's poems are often concise and "interweave the varied and numerous antagonisms inherent in lived experience" - Bob Beagrie, Lecturer Teesside University.

"Only Rumour Survives" is David's fourth collection.

New Contexts: 1 & New Contexts: 2

Globally the number of people being creative with language is truly extraordinary. While each of us will have our individual reasons for writing, many of them common, where the majority come together is in the desire to be read.

There are lots of outlets for writers, contributing to an ever-expanding and increasingly densely populated literary landscape, and people continue to submit to competitions, journals and magazines. In the vast majority of cases we do so not for financial reward but for recognition, to be validated, to have a 'readership'.

When it comes to publication, of the two deciding factors - talent and luck - the latter is the most fickle.

The idea for *New Contexts* was born from all of the above. The goal, to harvest a small sample of good unpublished writing and create an anthology to showcase it.

Joyriding Down Utopia Avenue by Simon French

"Readers of Simon French's debut collection *Joyriding Down Utopia Avenue* are in a for a delightfully jolt-filled, dodgem-car ride. People search for thrills, only to find them deflating into disillusionment. Yet elsewhere there are tender, moving and funny encounters in suburbia. Turns and twists of perspective abound, surprising, often shocking and sometimes mystifying us. What we thought we had experienced shifts dramatically, and we need to re-think what we have witnessed.

"The ride may be occasionally bumpy but French has a firm grasp of his wheel. His forms are spare, pared down, and his sensuous descriptive skills and playful wit excite the ear. He has a beady eye for focussing on details that make his places and subjects become vividly present. Happiness may be rare, hard-won, but the verbal fun and psychological thoughtfulness on offer means that riding with French down Utopia Avenue is never dull and more than joyful." - Jim Friedman

She Who Sings Is Not Always Happy by Julia Usman

"Julia Usman's poetry invites us into her childhood landscape of farm and meadows, schooldays, and travels in France, Brussels, Milan and beyond. It is poetry at ease in all those environments. Her close observations and reflections are delicately woven into 'Finding a voice', 'Still Life' and many more. This is a collection deeply layered with longing and grace for people loved and times gone, poetry I want to read again and again. Beautiful." - Kerry Darbishire

"Julia Usman's poetry ranges from inner landscape to outer; through memories of her own childhood, growing up on a farm in her beloved Yorkshire, woven through with memories of others. They are deeply rooted in place, yet her sensitive observations of people and place also travel. The poems sing of joy and loss; of pain and beauty. Her poems are spare and clear, they remind me of spring water, yet they allow breathing space for the reader to enter. Whether read individually, or as a whole, this collection is of its time, yet timeless. A collection to savour." - Geraldine Green

On Parliament Hill by Ian Gouge

Her voice is a trigger; a voice which forces Neil to relive the crises and failures of his past, and which offers him the possibility of a positive new future. But before he can decide on what he wants the life ahead of him to look like - and her role in it - he must pass judgement on himself.

Ian Gouge's novels focus on individuals who are trying to come to terms with their histories; characters facing a struggle, legacies from which they have to find a way to free themselves.

The Homelessness of a Child by Ian Gouge

By the time Ian Gouge went to university he had already lived in seventeen different places - houses, pre-fabs, flats, rooms of one sort or another - and all within the environs of the same two towns on the south coast of England. No single location more than four miles from the next, between some you could have measured the distance in hundreds of yards.

A number of these accommodations had been emergency refuges provided by the Local Authority to stave off homelessness, but in reality, every single residence proved temporary. Exactly at a time when a child needed security, the very notions of 'home', 'family' - even 'love' - were being challenged, their meanings redefined, shaken to their core; experiences which scarred both an upbringing and the future which followed it.

In the major thread of *The Homelessness of a Child*, the poet reflects on that childhood, explores its events and repercussions. Inevitably it is both a passionate and dispassionate retelling, the latter a result of the detachment a young boy would learn to adopt in order to protect himself from the chaos of the world he was forced to inhabit.

Pins & Feathers by Kate Miller, Emma Blowers, Erin Thompson

Coverstory books is thrilled to be bringing to market its first collection of plays. These three plays, all produced by Hertfordshire-based community theatre 'Pins & Feathers', tell extraordinary stories of ordinary people. With emotion and humour, they bring history to life, portraying characters challenged by events beyond their control, whose defiant voices resonate today.

- **The Last Witch**, by Kate Miller
- **Seeing it Through**, by Kate Miller, Emma Blowers and Erin Thompson
- **The March**, by Kate Miller

Stepping Westward by Berta Lawrence

The hill country of West Somerset is famous for its association with the Romantic poets, Coleridge and Wordsworth, whose *Lyrical Ballads* (1798) emerged out of their experience of the area and revolutionised English poetry. It was 130 years later that a young teacher, Berta Lawrence, came to live in the same part of the county.

Over the next seventy years, inspired by its landscape and legends, she wrote a succession of books and novels. She also wrote poems, over fifty of which were published in a local journal. After her death, more than two hundred poems were discovered among her papers, some published, some in typescript, and some in hand-written drafts. Here for the first time *Stepping Westward* gathers up the best of these, critically edited by Tom Furniss. They show how the storied Somerset landscape and the natural cycle of its rural year continue to inspire and delight.